Davy Crockett

Young Rifleman

Illustrated by Justin Pearson

Davy Crockett

Young Rifleman

by Aileen Wells Parks

Aladdin Paperbacks

Aladdin Paperbacks
An imprint of Simon & Schuster
Children's Publishing Division
1230 Avenue of the Americas
New York, NY 10020
Copyright © 1949, 1962, 1983 by the Bobbs-Merrill Co., Inc.

First Aladdin Paperbacks edition, 1986
Printed in the United States of America

30 29 28 27 26 25

Library of Congress Cataloging-in-Publication Data

Parks, Aileen Wells.
  Davy Crockett, young rifleman.

  Reprint of the edition: Indianapolis : Bobbs-Merrill,
c1983.
  Summary: A biography of the famous frontiersman and
Congressman, focusing on his childhood.
  1. Crockett, Davy, 1786–1836—Childhood and youth—
Juvenile literature. 2. Pioneers—Tennessee—Biography—
Juvenile literature. [1. Crockett, Davy, 1786–1836.
2. Pioneers. 3. Legislators] I. Pearson, Justin, ill.
II. Title.
F436.C95P37 1986   976.8'04'0924 [B] [92]   86-10781
ISBN-13: 978-0-02-041840-5
ISBN-10: 0-02-041840-X

For Jim
and
for young Jimmy

Illustrations

Numerous smaller illustrations

Contents

CHILDHOOD
OF FAMOUS
® · AMERICANS

★   ★   ★

Books by Aileen Wells Parks

BEDFORD FORREST: HORSEBACK BOY
DAVY CROCKETT: YOUNG RIFLEMAN
JAMES OGLETHORPE: YOUNG DEFENDER

★Davy Crockett

Young Rifleman

Davy's First Haircut

Mrs. Crockett was firm. "Every boy and man on this Tennessee clearing gets a haircut this day. You are all as shaggy as Indian colts after a hard winter."

Seven-year-old Davy looked at his four older brothers. Long hair hung around the ears and down the neck of each one. It had felt warm and comfortable all winter. Not even Pa had had a haircut since fall.

There was sunlight in the main room of the log cabin. Outside the spring sun was warm. The heavy front door stood wide open. The wooden shutters on the two square windows were fastened back. Except for the backlog, there were only live coals on the big hearth.

Davy nudged eight-year-old Wilson. "Come on, Willy. We'll be wild ponies and Ma can't catch us."

"You will be right here when your turns come, Davy and Wilson. Clear out now till I get through with the big ones."

Davy and Willy, with little Joe tagging after them, cantered into the yard. They galloped and they bucked. They neighed and they whinnied. They shook their manes and kicked up their heels. Around and around the bare space near the house, down the slope to the edge of Limestone Creek, the make-believe horses raced and played.

Soon they grew lazy and came back to the yard to watch the haircutting.

Ma had chosen a big stump near the house for her barber chair. First Pa was seated there to have his hair cut. Then Jason, Jim, and Bill each took his turn.

Ma placed the pewter bowl she had brought all the way from Maryland over each head in turn. Her shears had come from Maryland, too, and Ma was very proud of them. The blades were heavy and long. Pa or Jason honed them sharp for her, but Ma always stood by to see that they did the job right.

Davy and Wilson laughed and teased the older boys. Grown-up Polly and little Janie, glad that girls could wear long hair, came out to watch and laugh, too.

"Jason's got a haircut! Jason's got a haircut!" they chanted. "Jason can't fight. Jason's too white under his ears!"

"Ma, Jim's ears are too big."

"Look, Ma, old Whirlwind's just waiting to eat a piece of Jim's big ear."

"Watch out, Jim! She's a-cutting!"

13

Bill didn't fidget. He hunched up his shoulders and shut his eyes. He held his head so still the bowl didn't move.

"Bill's a scaredy! Bill's a scaredy!"

The older boys did not stay after Ma let them go. They followed Pa to the creek. Long before it was Davy's turn they were splashing and yelling in the cool water.

Davy begged, "Please, Ma, cut my hair tomorrow. Look, Ma, let me go swimming now and tomorrow I'll sit just as still as Bill did."

Ma would not listen—just put the bowl on Davy's head. The bowl was too big, and she sent Janie to get a smaller gourd bowl.

The shears looked bigger and brighter and sharper close up. They made a great clacking noise. When the cold metal touched his ear Davy gave a yell and jumped. He would have run away, but Ma had a firm grip on his head.

"Sit still, Davy. I haven't cut off an ear yet."

14

The big shears clicked above Davy's ears and
across the back of his head. Their flat blades felt
cold against his scalp as Ma clipped the long hair
away.

Then Ma took the bowl from Davy's head and combed his hair with the coarse-toothed wooden comb. She trimmed the longer hair on top of his head.

"Ma, there's hair on my face and down my neck! It itches!"

"Be still, Davy," Ma said. "You've fidgeted more than all the rest put together."

"Ma, that's enough. Ma! I don't want to look like a skinned possum."

"You won't, Davy," Polly said with a laugh. "You look more like a coon with its hair all roughed up."

Davy made a face at her. Wilson, who was waiting for him, suddenly shouted, "Davy grins just like a coon."

Janie came up and peered into Davy's face. "Do you?" she asked. "Do it now. I want to see how a coon grins."

Davy looked at her round little face and

couldn't help laughing. "Sure, Janie. I can grin better than any coon that ever lived." He gave her a wide grin.

Polly and Ma laughed. Ma combed his hair once more and then laid down the shears. "Go on, boys. Pa's got the soap. Wash well."

Pa, with Jason and Jim, was already out of the water. They sat on a big rock in the sun getting dry. Bill watched Wilson and Davy rub soap on their bare bodies. The harsh lye soap made the boys' skin tingle.

"That's enough. Come on now. Let's see if you've forgotten how to swim."

Wilson jumped in. "Br-r-r! It's cold!" He thrashed around to get warm.

Bill splashed water on Davy. "Jump in, Davy, and work like Willy. It's fine."

Davy held his breath and threw himself flat on the water. His arms and legs moved violently, almost before he thought. Bill had taught him to dog-paddle the summer before, but this was no time for such a slow stroke.

"Hey, Willy! Who said this water was cold?" Davy was warming up.

After a bit the three boys climbed on a rock in the center of the stream. The sunny rock felt warm, but the air was chilly. Davy started to go down toward the pool on the other side.

Suddenly Pa yelled, "Davy Crockett, get back on that rock!"

When Pa spoke all the boys heeded. He demanded prompt obedience. He didn't hesitate to use a whip if he didn't get it fast enough.

Davy climbed back. Pa added, "Don't you dare go swimming in that big pool. The current is mighty strong in there when the creek is full. It would take you right on down over the falls and out into the Nolichucky River. You'd be drowned sure. I don't want to see any of you boys trying to swim there."

When Davy got dressed, his clean linsey trousers and shirt felt good. The air was cool against his neck. He felt slim and tall and grown-up. He felt big enough to climb old Bald Mountain, or kill a brown bear, or paddle a canoe down the Tennessee River. He wanted to run and climb trees and shout at the top of his voice.

The spring night was chilly. It was good, after supper, to sit on stools or on the floor around the big hearth fire.

Pa told tales, fine ones, about Noah building an ark when the big freshet came; about a man named Samson who had more strength than any man in the world, till his hair was cut.

Then he told about fighting Indians. Pa knew many Indian stories. When he and his father had moved over the Smoky Mountains in 1775, Indians had hunted through all these woods. They had tried to drive out the white farmers to protect their hunting grounds. They had killed and scalped Grandpa and Grandmother Crockett and carried off Pa's younger brother.

All that had happened several years before Davy was born in 1786. Pa had helped to drive the Indians out of this part of the valley and to the south along the great bend of the Tennessee River.

After he finished telling about the Indians, Pa told about Daniel Boone on a bear hunt.

"When I'm big I'm going hunting with Daniel Boone," Jim said. "Daniel Boone's the best hunter in Carolina or Virginia or Kentucky or anywhere else."

Jason said he was going to learn how to make guns. A man had to have a good gun to hunt with, and Jason wanted to make them.

Davy was staring into the flames. Polly nudged him gently. "What are you going to be when you grow up, Davy?" she asked.

Davy didn't turn around. "I'm going to be six feet tall," he told the fire.

Everyone laughed. Davy flushed and his hard little hands doubled into fists.

"I'm going to hunt, too," he said determinedly. "I bet I kill more bears than anyone else, even Daniel Boone."

Adventure in the Forest

ONE SUNNY DAY in early summer Davy was lonesome. Pa had given all the other boys jobs to do.

Ma and Polly were busy, too. Janie had to rock the heavy cradle so tiny baby Sarah would not cry. Little Joe was sound asleep.

Davy wandered up the hill. A big hound was lying half in the shade, half in the sun. Davy called, "Here, Whirlwind, here. Come here, Whirly."

The dog cocked one ear and looked around lazily. He did not get up. He didn't even stretch.

"Best bear dog in all the Great Smoky Mountains," Pa often said. "Give me old Whirlwind and I can tree any bear that ever grew. He has more sense than most men."

"Come on, Whirlwind. Get up." Davy pulled the dog's ear. "Let's go hunt bear."

Whirlwind growled softly. He might have been dreaming.

Davy poked at him. "Bear, Whirlwind. Bear!" He tried to make his voice deep like his father's voice, but without success.

This time Whirlwind got up and stretched. He did not jump around and bark as he did when Pa said, "Bear!"

Davy started up the path toward the forest. Whirlwind followed. He looked slow and lazy, but he kept up with the boy. Davy talked to him. "We'll go right up this path. Then we come to the trail. Bill showed me one time. It starts at the big sycamore tree where Pa got the wildcat."

Whirlwind yawned loudly. Davy looked back. The hound seemed ready to stop and finish his nap.

"Come on, Whirlwind. Here, boy, here!" Davy picked up a stick, held it before the dog, and then threw it up the path as hard as he could throw.

Whirlwind looked at him with disdain. That was puppy play.

Then Davy remembered. He would need a stick in case he met a bear. Looking for a good strong stick, he left the path. Soon he found a kind of trail which led like a tunnel through the underbrush.

It was fun to go through the tunnel. It turned now to the right and now to the left. Sometimes sunlight came through the leaves. Sometimes the tunnel was almost dark. Davy forgot he was looking for a stick. He pretended that he was a fox trailing an opossum.

His bare feet made no noise on the path. He brushed the little branches away from his face as quietly as he could. Often the tunnel was so low he had to crawl.

After a long time he came out beside a rocky ledge. Davy climbed up and lay down to rest. He watched the sun on the leaves over his head. Then he fell sound asleep.

When he woke up he thought Wilson was pushing him out of their bed. He kicked back. His foot hit soft fur. Since he slept under a fur covering all winter long that felt right.

Then something cold touched his face. Davy threw up his hand and hit the rug again, but this time the rug felt different. Davy opened his eyes and looked behind him.

A little bear cub was sitting quietly on the rock beside him.

The bear seemed friendly. It wrinkled up its nose and sniffed at Davy. It looked at him out of bright black eyes. Then it put its nose down on his hand.

It was a cold nose and Davy jumped. When he suddenly sat up, the cub moved back. It was such a cute little thing scuttling away on all fours that Davy laughed.

The cub must have liked the sound of Davy's laugh. It stopped and turned to look back.

Davy held out his hand. "I bet I could make a pet out of you," he said.

The little bear wrinkled its nose at him again. Then it sat down and watched Davy. The boy got to his feet to go over to it.

Just as he moved, Davy heard a snort. It was a scary sort of sound. Davy stood very still. He did not dare even to look around.

There was another snort. This time Davy looked up. A large brown bear was watching him out of little, beady eyes. Its mouth was open. Its big red tongue hung out.

The sight surprised Davy so much that he screamed. He looked around to find a place to run. The only open space he could see was across the rocky ledge. There were big trees on the other side with few bushes under them.

Davy tried to slip away. The big bear started moving, too. Davy was watching so closely he slipped on some loose gravel. He grabbed up a handful of the small pebbles and flung them straight at the two bears.

The mother might have caught him then, but the little bear whimpered. The big bear stopped quickly and went to her baby.

Davy, on one knee, saw the mother nuzzle the little bear. He jumped up and ran. Under the trees he turned to look back. The mother bear was watching him. She was in front of the cub.

Davy did want that cub for a pet. "I'd call him Bear Hug," he thought.

The bear must have understood. She glared and growled and then took a step forward. Davy saw her long red tongue lick out. "G-r-r-r," the bear said again. She stretched out a forepaw and raked her claws over the rock. The claws were like a cat's, but they were bigger and longer. The scratch left white gashes on the rock.

Davy kept his eye on the bear but began backing down the hill. That growl had made his heart beat fast. Then he stepped on a branch which crackled loudly.

The sound startled the bear and she moved toward the boy. Not even her baby's tiny growl stopped her this time. She was headed straight for Davy.

Davy turned and ran as fast as he could go. The woods were clear, and the way was slightly downhill, but the big bear, growling deep in her throat, ran faster than Davy could.

Davy felt a scream burst from his throat. Then he closed his mouth tight to keep all his breath for running.

He could hear the bear behind him. He thought he felt hot breath on the back of his neck. He ran faster.

Then a root, sticking up from the ground, tripped him. He fell and rolled over and over down a steep place on the hill.

The bear was running so fast she went right past where Davy lay, but she did not go far. She turned, and Davy saw her beady eyes, red now with anger, as she came toward him.

Suddenly there was a great barking. The bear turned its head, then its whole body, to face this unexpected sound.

It was Whirlwind. The dog was making enough noise for a whole pack of bearhounds. He jumped from side to side of the angry bear. He barked right in her face but kept out of reach of her powerful paws. Her long claws were bared as she grabbed for the dog.

By circling, Whirlwind forced the bear to retreat. When she moved toward Davy, the dog dashed forward to nip her.

Davy was too scared to move.

The dog would circle toward one side and the bear would circle facing him. When he was even with her and threatening to go past, she would growl and attack. As Whirlwind raced back and around to the other side, she moved back, step by step.

Davy looked up the hill. There was the cub, watching with as much interest as Davy.

The mother also saw the cub. She began backing steadily up the hill. Her angry eyes watched Whirlwind, but she did not try to attack him now. The hound kept up a great fury of barking and running, but he was not pressing the attack as hard as he had at first.

Finally the mother bear reached her cub. She and the dog stood feet apart, growling threats at each other.

Suddenly the two bears were gone in the leafy forest. Davy was amazed that they could disappear so fast.

Whirlwind came back and stood by the boy. He was panting hard.

Just then Mr. Crockett came up the hill, with his rifle ready in his hands. "Davy! Davy!" he was shouting.

"Here I am, Pa!" Davy called.

"You all right, Davy?"

"Pa, you should have seen old Whirlwind drive that bear back up that hill!" Davy forgot he had ever been scared. "Pa, will you give Whirlwind to me for my bearhound?"

Mr. Crockett studied the boy. "When you get big enough to hunt bear you may have him for your very own," he promised.

Davy's First Deer Hunt

"Ma," called Davy excitedly one day. "Here comes Uncle Joe."

Mrs. Crockett straightened up from her loom. Her brother, Joseph Hawkins, came in through the open door.

"How are you, Joe? The red rooster stood on the top step to crow this morning. I've been expecting somebody."

"Morning, Rebecca. John or Jason here?"

"Why, no. Jason and his pa are over to Woody's. They've just put in a new water wheel and Jason's helping grind out gunpowder. What do you want?"

"We're about out of meat at our house and I'm going after a deer. Two people can hunt better than one. Jim around?"

"Oh, Ma," broke in Davy, "let me go with Uncle Joe. Please, Ma!"

"You're too fidgety to hunt deer, Davy." Mrs. Crockett's voice was sharp. "Keep quiet now. Let me think. Jim went——"

Davy stepped up to his Uncle Joe. "I know deer tracks, Uncle Joe. I can be awfully quiet in the woods, too."

Uncle Joe shook his head, but Davy kept on. "Besides, I've just naturally got to learn how to hunt. I'm almost a man and I don't know how yet."

"Gunpowder is pretty scarce, Davy." Uncle Joe put his hand on the boy's head. Then he grinned. "Get on some deerskin breeches and we'll see if you are growing into a woodsman or just a man."

Davy scampered up the ladder into the loft before his mother could object. When he came down again a few minutes later he was wearing jacket, trousers, and moccasins of deerskin. Briers and thickets couldn't hurt these clothes.

Uncle Joe reached for the long rifle he had stood against the cabin wall. "I'll take care of the boy, Rebecca," he said. "We'll not go as far as Piney. We'll be back before sundown."

Davy walked carefully. He tried to match his steps to his uncle's long stride. He made more noise because he was watching his uncle instead of leaves and twigs on the ground.

At first Uncle Joe did not notice. They were on the path near the house and there was little need to take care in walking.

"Walk toe first, Davy. That's the way the Indians do. See, like this." He set his toe lightly and let his heel down gently but firmly.

The trail back into the forest was narrow.

Davy walked behind his uncle. Now that he couldn't try to match steps with him, he walked more easily.

They followed an old trail that buffaloes had made coming to Limestone Creek for water. Uncle Joe wasn't looking for deer yet. The shy animals rarely came to Limestone now. The best place to find them was several miles away, along the lower slopes of Pine Mountain.

The trail led around the knob of a small hill. When Davy and Uncle Joe came to an open place, they stopped to rest. From here they could see out over the country. To the left were two layers of mountains in the distance. They were outlined hazily against the sky, and they looked smoky-blue, not green. To the right was Pine Mountain. It was near enough for Davy to see that it was covered to the top with trees.

Uncle Joe turned to go on, but Davy caught his coat.

"Look, Uncle Joe," he whispered. "See those grapevines over there."

Uncle Joe looked in the direction Davy was pointing. Some fifty yards away there was a heavy growth of wild grapevines. The matted vines were so thick that nothing could be seen through them.

The vines moved, but their movement was not caused by the light breeze.

Uncle Joe and Davy watched, trying hard to see through the heavy leaves.

Sometimes they could see a tiny flash of something tawny. Whatever it was, it would reach up, grab the vine, and pull down. Breathlessly Davy watched. It must be a deer eating grapes. Pa said deer loved them.

He and Uncle Joe had seen no deer tracks on the trail, but there were many ways for deer to get into a thicket like that. Again and again the tawny head reached up and grabbed grapes from the vine. The vine would shake, snap, shake again, and be still.

Uncle Joe opened his powder horn. He poured some powder down the long barrel. He placed a small round ball of lead in a tiny patch of well-greased doeskin. With his ram-rod, he pushed the patch and the bullet down the barrel on top of the powder.

Davy watched first his uncle, then the thicket. Uncle Joe was taking such a long time to get ready! Now the vines were still. Had the deer caught their scent and gone away? Davy was almost sick with disappointment.

Uncle Joe took a step to one side and rested the long barrel of his rifle on the branch of a small tree. He watched the vine and waited. Davy held his breath and watched, too.

Then they saw the tawny form once more. Uncle Joe pulled the trigger. There was a flash and a loud, sharp, cracking noise.

Immediately came another noise—a loud yell. Davy was surprised. He had not expected to hear a deer cry out.

There was a thrashing about in the vines. A hand pulled them apart suddenly and a man's head appeared.

"Hey, you!" the man shouted. "What do you mean shooting like that? You've killed me sure as moonshine."

Uncle Joe was so startled he almost dropped his gun. He set it carefully against a tree and ran toward the man. Davy was already on his way to the thicket. He knew the man. His name was Kendall and he lived in a clearing on the other side of Limestone Creek.

When Davy got there, Mr. Kendall was holding one hand tight against his shoulder. Blood was oozing between his fingers.

Mr. Kendall was angry and he was talking fast and loud. Davy hardly heard what he said.

39

"A man can't even gather grapes without some crazy fellow shooting daylight through him. You've killed me, Joe Hawkins. You come through the woods blowing off your gun as though you have no sense at all. Not a bit. Joe Hawkins, you must have a lot of powder and lead to waste to go around shooting at your neighbors. Don't you even look at what you're aiming at? You idiot, you crazy——"

Uncle Joe said, "Well, I guess you aren't dead yet if you can talk that much."

Mr. Kendall kept on. "You drilled me clean through. There's blood a-trickling down my back. Of all the crazy——"

"I thought it was a deer in here, eating grapes. Why didn't you whistle or shout or something? Didn't you see us standing over there in the opening?"

Mr. Kendall was too angry to answer questions. "I'm a dying man and you just stand there staring at me. Do something, you idiot, before I die!"

Uncle Joe said, "Reckon you can make out to walk home, Dick? We can't do much for you up here."

Mr. Kendall took his hands away, and Uncle Joe looked at the holes in his jacket. There were dark red patches on the front and back, about three inches below the shoulder. The spots got bigger as Davy watched.

Uncle Joe collected some leaves. He placed these very gently inside Mr. Kendall's jacket over the blood in front and back.

"That should hold the flow if we go down carefully," he said. "Take it easy now, Dick. Keep your left arm tight across your chest like that. Now hold onto me with the other."

He reached down and picked up the wooden bucket Mr. Kendall had filled with grapes.

"Davy, you go get my rifle and bring it

down. Mind how you carry it down. Easy now, Dick. Let's take it easy."

Davy went down the path in front. He was pleased that Uncle Joe trusted him to carry the long, heavy rifle.

He stepped carefully, holding the stock tightly against his shoulder. It took both hands to keep it steady. When he got tired walking like that he tried holding the rifle lengthwise, but that was awkward. He could hardly keep the barrel from trailing on the ground.

Finally he held the gun at an angle in front of him, his right hand on the stock, his left steadying the heavy barrel. It wasn't easy, but Davy was proud to be carrying a rifle.

The boy reached home first. His father was in the yard and Davy called to him. "Pa! Pa! Uncle Joe shot——"

Mr. Crockett did not let him finish. "Joe shot himself? Where is he? How did it happen?

Here, put that gun down, boy! We've got to go help Uncle Joe."

"Not Uncle Joe, Pa," Davy said. "Uncle Joe shot Mr. Kendall. They're coming now."

Mr. Crockett had already started up the path.

Davy placed the rifle carefully on the porch against the wall where nothing could happen to it. "Don't you let little Joe touch Uncle Joe's gun," he cautioned Janie.

In a few moments Mr. Crockett came running back. "Rebecca," he called to Mrs. Crockett, "where's that silk handkerchief Grandpa brought from Ireland? And where's the pepper and some hot water? Hurry, Rebecca. Joe's shot Dick Kendall and it's bad."

Davy's mother rushed about getting things ready. The older boys—Jason, Jim, Bill, and Wilson—came running. The hounds barked loudly at the excitement.

When Uncle Joe and Mr. Kendall came, Pa

was all ready. The pail of hot water was on the floor near the edge of the porch. Pa made Mr. Kendall sit down on a stump near by.

"Get back out of my way, boys!" he shouted.

Davy stayed on the porch where he could keep a hand on the rifle. He watched Pa cut away Mr. Kendall's jacket with Ma's big shears. With a clean cloth dipped in hot water Pa washed the bloodstained leaves away. The holes in Mr. Kendall's skin were small, neat circles just below the shoulder bone.

"You are lucky, Dick. It didn't hit a bone. Just went through the flesh."

Pa picked up the fine silk handkerchief. He wrapped it carefully around a slender knitting needle Ma handed him. He sprinkled black pepper generously along it.

"Now, Dick, this is going to hurt more than a mite, but you can stand it. Joe, you hold him tight on that side. Move back out of the way, boys. Here, Jason, you hang onto this arm. Brace yourself, Dick, and keep as still as you can."

With a steady pressure Pa sent the needle and the handkerchief through the bullet hole. Mr. Kendall gritted his teeth so hard his lips pulled back. Sweat broke out over his face in great drops, but he didn't make a sound.

Davy let his breath out slowly, as the handkerchief was drawn all the way through.

Wilson was sitting on the ground watching. Jim and Bill came up on the porch. Davy moved back by the rifle. Polly came out with more hot water and clean rags for bandages.

"You'd better keep Janie and Joe in the house," Davy told her. "They might try to touch Uncle Joe's rifle, and they're not big enough."

Christmas Eve

CHRISTMAS EVE was cold. A strong wind whistled down the valley. Two days before, the milk cow had disappeared from the pasture near the woods. Pa had given her up for lost. Probably bears or wolves had eaten her, he said. Then a neighbor had come by and said that Old Bossy had strayed and was several miles away with Mr. Bowman's cows.

Ma said, "Well, that's a blessing to hear and a load off my mind. We'll send for her this very day. We need that cow."

Then she hesitated. Mr. Bowman's clearing was somewhere on Little Beaver Creek. It was even farther from the main trail than the Crockett cabin. It must be four miles away. Pa and the older boys were in the woods. Wilson had gone with Polly to carry food to the Kendall family who lived close by.

"Ma, I can go get Old Bossy," Davy urged.

"You'd get lost. Besides, you couldn't drive than cantankerous beast home by yourself."

"I can find the way, Ma. I can take the horse bridle to put around her neck and lead her. If she gets balky, I'll howl like a wolf."

Ma laughed and gave in. She needed the milk. She dressed Davy warmly and let him go.

He followed a path through the cane. In summer and fall it was shady and pleasant. Now the wind whistled down the trail. Heavy gusts caught the stiff, leafless canes and whipped them across the path, striking Davy's body and face.

He pulled his coonskin cap close about his

ears and beat his cold red hands against his chest. The wind tugged at his buckskin suit.

Davy tried to sing. He started a song Pa often sang, "We'll rally in the canebrake, boys, and shoot the buffalo." The wind rushed down his throat. It drowned out the sound, even to himself. He could not even keep his lips puckered to whistle.

It was colder outdoors than he had thought it would be, and farther—much farther. The ground was hard underfoot. He could feel the frozen ridges through his heavy moccasins.

At a fork in the trail Davy stopped. He could not remember which path to take. With relief he thought, "I'm lost. I can go back and tell Ma I couldn't find the way." The cold wind would be whistling at his back, not his face. There would be a roaring fire waiting for him and a big bowl of hot cornmeal mush.

There would be no milk with the mush,

though. Davy couldn't guess what Ma would say, or Pa either. Maybe Pa wouldn't let him shoot tomorrow. On Christmas Day Pa always let the big boys shoot his rifle. Last year neither Davy nor Wilson had been allowed to shoot.

Davy turned his back to the wind and blew on his cold hands. If he ran home fast maybe Ma wouldn't tell he had ever started. Still, she would have to tell Pa to send to Mr. Bowman's for Old Bossy. Then Pa would say, "Why didn't you send Davy? Was he too little to find the way to the Bowmans' place?"

Suddenly Davy remembered some words Uncle Joe had once said: "Be sure you're right and go ahead." He had started after Bossy. He would take her home.

The trail had turned from the canebrake along the creek. The left fork climbed a steep ridge. The right fork led down along the foot of the ridge.

50

Mr. Bowman lived at the foot of a hill. Was it this hill, or would Davy have to go up this hill and across to another?

In the fall Davy, with Jim and Bill and Wilson, had passed Mr. Bowman's house when they were hunting nuts. They had talked to him, then wandered on until they reached the river. They had been in the woods all day. Davy had never gone directly to Mr. Bowman's cabin.

He looked down the two trails, and tried to remember how the clearing had looked. He recalled that the house was a one-room log cabin with a wattle chimney of sticks and dirt at one end. A spring was a little way up the hill and the water ran down to a small creek. The sun had been shining that fall day, and the cabin was in the shade of the hill.

If the sun were shining now it would be on the other side of the hill. Davy took the right-hand path. Soon this path, too, climbed a bit, then dipped and curved around a knob of the hill. There in front of him was the very clearing he remembered! There was the big chestnut tree between the cabin and the spring.

Davy broke into a run. The latchstring on the door was on the outside and the boy gave it a hearty tug. As the heavy door opened at his pull, Davy shouted, "Hey, Mr. Bowman! I've come for Old Bossy."

Two men were sitting by the blazing fire. The other side of the room was in deep shadow. One man was Mr. Bowman. The other had a violin and was playing and singing as Davy rushed in. He didn't even look up.

"Come in, boy, and shut that door quick," said Mr. Bowman. "I guess you are one of the Crocketts. Which one are you?"

"I'm Davy, sir."

"Well, Davy, come up close to the fire and thaw out."

The hot fire made Davy's hands and face burn. He had to draw back from the hearth.

His whole body tingled from the sudden heat.

The man with the violin stared at him but did not say a word. He kept on playing softly, patting time with his foot.

"Here, Davy, take a sip of this tea. It will drive out the cold." Mr. Bowman held out a gourd cup.

Davy swallowed some of the bitter leaf brew. It made his mouth and throat burn. Soon he felt warm all through.

The music sounded nice, but the fire made him sleepy. He wanted to lean back against the chimney corner and listen till he fell asleep. However, he had come for Old Bossy, and he must be taking her back.

"Thank you very much, sir," he told Mr. Bowman. He handed back the cup. "I reckon I'd better be getting home."

"Not in this wind tonight, boy. It's blowing for a blizzard. You'd get lost."

"It will be easier going back. I told Ma I'd bring Old Bossy and I'd better go."

Mr. Bowman got up and went out to the cowpen with Davy. He had two oxen and a milk cow. These three, with Bossy, were huddled in one corner of the enclosure where the tall, close-set stakes cut the wind.

Bossy did not want to leave, but Davy drove her out and tied the bridle around her horns.

"That's a bad way to take a cow most times," Mr. Bowman said, "but I reckon you'll have no trouble going toward home."

As they got to the path, the musician was coming out the door. He was so wrapped up in shawls and blankets that Davy could hardly recognize him.

"I figure I'll go 'long with the lad, Ben," he said to Mr. Bowman.

"I hate to lose your company, Jasper," Mr. Bowman said. "You'll have a fine Christmas with the Crocketts, though. Wait a minute. With you to help mind the cow, Davy can take a piggin of chestnuts to Miss Polly and her ma."

Jasper, carrying his violin and the piggin of nuts, was only a little help to Davy. At first Old Bossy was balky. She tried to turn back to the shelter of the cowpen.

Davy found a stout stick by the side of the path. First tugging at the bridle, then poking the cow from behind, he urged her along. Jasper barred the path and whooped at her when she tried to turn.

Once around the knob of the hill, the wind was at their backs. With Jasper guarding the rear, Davy was able to lead Old Bossy homeward at a lively pace.

When they reached the path through the canebrake, Bossy showed more interest in getting home. Davy took the bridle from her horns and went back to walk with Jasper.

The rest of the way seemed short. Jasper was jolly and knew a lot of riddles. He asked Davy, "Why does a dog wag his tail?"

Davy guessed as hard as he could, but Jasper finally had to tell him the answer: "Because the tail can't wag the dog!"

Then Davy asked Jasper, "What goes all over the hills but doesn't eat? What goes to the creek but doesn't drink?"

Jasper had heard that one. "A cowbell. You should know this one, Davy. What is it goes uphill and downhill, stands still all the time, but goes to mill every day?"

Davy objected, "If it stands still, it can't go to mill every day."

"Why not? You can't and a horse can't, but a path can."

Then Jasper asked, "What is it goes on four legs in the morning, on two legs at noon, and on three at night?"

Davy had no idea what Jasper meant.

"Why, it's a baby crawling around on all fours in the morning," Jasper said with a laugh. "When he's grown up he's a man walking on two legs, and at night he's an old man using a stick."

Davy could hardly wait to try the new riddles on Wilson. All except the one about the legs, that is. That one was good enough to try on Pa, he thought.

All the family were home when Davy arrived with Old Bossy and Jasper. They were glad to have a guest.

"Why, Jasper Beale," boomed Pa, "I haven't seen you in years. Where you been keeping yourself?"

"It will be just like Christmas in the settlements," Ma said, "to have music in the house."

After supper Pa suddenly interrupted Jasper's music. "Mighty kind of you to help Davy home with the cow, Jasper."

"Davy brought the cow, John," Jasper answered. "I just came along."

Jasper played a few measures of a familiar song. "Here's a new verse," he said. He played a few notes, then sang:

" 'Oh, what can you do, Davy boy, Davy boy,
    Oh, what can you do, John Davy?'
    'I can hunt, and I can plow,
    I can drive a balky cow,
    I'm a big boy and just like my pappy.' "

Christmas Day

THERE WAS snow on the ground when Davy woke up Christmas morning. However, the wind had died down and it wasn't so cold as it had been the day before.

Davy was down from the loft as soon as he heard his father poke up the backlog and add new wood to the fire. "Pa, it's Christmas Day. I reckon it's about time to shoot the rifle."

"Boy, its mighty early in the day to talk about shooting. Why, it isn't light yet."

Davy was the first one to finish breakfast. "Pa, I'll just wait outside till it's time to shoot."

Wilson jumped up. "Wait for me, Davy.

Wait for me. I get to shoot this year, don't I, Pa? Davy's not old enough, is he, Pa?"

Ma interrupted. "Eat your breakfast, Wilson. Don't tease your pa."

"I get first turn, Pa," Jim reminded his father. "You said I did."

The three boys were all talking at once. They surrounded their father, arguing with one another.

Mr. Crockett stood up abruptly. His quick Irish temper flared. "I'll take the skin off the next boy that says 'rifle' to me," he threatened. "We'll set up a target after dinner. Everybody will have his chance, starting with Jason and right down the line. Not a word till then!"

For weeks Davy had been counting the days till Christmas. Last year Pa had said he was too small to shoot the long heavy rifle. He hadn't even let Wilson shoot with the older boys. Ever since he had carried Uncle Joe's

rifle home from the woods, however, Davy had been sure Pa would let him shoot this year. Pa hadn't yet said he might shoot, but he hadn't said he couldn't.

Outside Wilson tried to explain to Davy that he wouldn't be old enough till next year. "I'm ten years old and you are just nine."

Davy lost his temper. He didn't say a word, but he doubled up his fists and hit his brother as hard as he could.

Caught off guard, Wilson slipped in the snow. Davy, carried forward by the force of his blow, sprawled in the snow, too. The two boys clinched and rolled. Fists flailed the air. Blows landed where they might.

Wilson was older and stronger, but the fight was just a scuffle to him. Davy fought because he was angry. Wilson could get him down, but he couldn't hold him. He could not control the hard fists that struck blindly.

Davy's fury finally pinned Wilson to the ground. His left elbow and body held him there. His right fist drew back. Davy was still fighting mad. He was in no humor to stop because his opponent was down.

Suddenly hard hands jerked him up. Jason was standing over the two boys. "Don't you know when to quit, youngster? You've got him down."

Davy hadn't fought out his anger. Tears blinded him. He strained in Jason's grip. "He said I couldn't shoot! I can, too! I'm going to!" His fist came up.

"You don't need a gun," Jason said. "You could whip any wildcat in the Smokies right now with your bare hands."

He picked up a handful of soft snow and rubbed it on Davy's face. "Cool off," he advised, "or Pa will lick you both. Here, Bill, let's roll these two panthers down the hill to the creek."

The older boys were rough, but it was play. Wilson and Davy wadded the damp snow into balls and threw it into their faces. Soon all the boys were laughing and scuffling together.

Dinner was late that day. The big pot hanging from the crane over the open fire held a venison roast. The air was full of its good odor. Turnips were stewing in a pot set over the coals, and hominy, too. Great pones of corn bread were cooking on iron platters set above live coals.

Davy was not hungry. At dinner he was too excited to eat. As soon as the meal was over, it would be time to shoot the rifle.

Jasper and Pa ate and talked, and talked and ate. Davy fidgeted on the long bench between Wilson and Bill.

Jasper was asking riddles again. "Houseful, yardful, can't catch a spoonful. What do you think it is?"

"I know what that is," said Ma. "It's the same thing that goes all over the house and never leaves a trace."

"Smoke!" chorused several Crocketts.

"Now, Jasper, you're a mighty good music maker, but do you know who the first musician was?" Pa asked.

Jasper looked puzzled.

"I'll tell you the kind of music he made," Pa went on. "He was a whistler."

Jasper laughed. "Of course! It was the wind. I reckon the first song he whistled was 'Over the hills and far away.'"

Davy was through eating long before anyone else. He got up and put on his coat and coonskin cap. "Pa, I'll wait outside," he announced as he went toward the door.

Mr. Crockett didn't hear him. Everybody else was too busy eating and listening to notice.

Outdoors Davy went to the target site. He

closed one eye and sighted along a stick as if it were the rifle. Whirlwind and two other hounds came around the house then. Davy raced and scuffled with them.

Finally Pa got ready. He fastened a good-sized scrap of bearskin to a large tree. The fur was against the bark. With the heated point of a poker he had drawn a crude diamond about ten inches long on the leather side. Lines from the corners crossed in the center.

Jason and Jim and Bill used the limb of a young tree nearly thirty yards from the target as a gun rest. Each boy shot once and each hit the target. Jason's shot was just above the center. Jim's was a bit high. Bill's was right in the left corner.

Davy grew more and more excited. He could hardly wait until his turn came to shoot, but Pa took his time.

Some ten feet nearer the target was a stump.

Pa set a small stool on the stump and balanced it carefully until it made a firm, steady rest. Then he placed the rifle on the stool and took careful sight. Satisfied at last, he signaled to his next son to come forward.

Wilson hung back. He was not really eager to handle the rifle. Davy impatiently took a step forward.

Pa said sharply, "Wilson!"

The boy went forward slowly. Pa placed his hands, one on the stock and one on the hammer. He braced the stock against Wilson's shoulder, steadied the heavy barrel. He said, "Now sight at the target and shoot."

Wilson, though he shut both eyes, was lucky. His shot hit the upper edge of the bearskin.

Davy was already close up, ready to take his place. The greatest moment of his life had come. As soon as Pa had poured in powder and rammed in the bullet Davy clutched the stock to his shoulder. He took hasty aim and pulled with all his might on the trigger.

A shrill *cr-r-ac-ck* sounded in his ears. The stock kicked against his shoulder, but he kept his feet planted firmly on the ground and his eyes fastened on the target.

Jason stepped nearer the tree to find the bullet mark. Bill went to help him. Jim said, "He missed as clean as a whistle." Pa shook his head and waited. He said nothing.

Davy gave the rifle to Pa and ran after Jason and Bill.

It was all wrong! He had missed. His shot was wide. It hadn't touched the target! It hadn't even touched the tree.

Davy was silent with a sense of complete failure. He had dreamed of the day he would surprise them all with a perfect shot on his first try, and he had missed even the tree! Wilson had nicked the target at least, but Davy, who wanted more than anything in the world to hunt, couldn't even hit a tree.

He turned away.

Bill looked down at him. "Better luck next year, boy," he said. "You just got in too big a hurry." He put his arm around Davy's shoulder, but the boy pulled away.

Jason went back toward his father. "Let's give the lad another try, Pa," he urged. "That was bad luck."

"I don't know. A shot apiece is the rule." Mr. Crockett eyed Davy's retreating figure. "Davy!" Mr. Crockett's voice was firm. The boy halted, then looked at his father. "I'd hate to have it said a Crockett couldn't even hit a tree. Come here and do that shot over again."

Davy's heart swelled till it was almost too big for his body. He walked toward his father, excited and happy. It was a second chance for which he had had no hope.

Mr. Crockett was stern. He explained carefully as he prepared the gun what Davy should do. He looked sharply at the boy's position. He made him sight the target carefully.

Davy was about to squeeze the trigger again when Mr. Crockett dropped his hand on the

boy's shoulder. "Wait a minute, son. You're as tense as a rattlesnake. Stand back a minute. Now tell me just what you're going to do."

Davy let his father take the gun from his hands. He looked the man squarely in the eyes.

"I'm going to put the stock tight against my shoulder. I'm going to hold her steady against the rest with one hand. I'm going to pull the hammer back with my other hand. Then I'm going to look right down that barrel till I set the sights on that big bear. And I'm going to get him square between the eyes."

Davy stepped up and grasped the rifle in both hands. He rested the barrel on the stool. He took steady aim, pulled the gun down slightly and fired.

There was another loud *cr-r-ac-ck*, and the explosion threw him back on his heels. He was deafened by the sound and blinded by smoke, but in spite of the jar he felt good inside.

Jason ran toward the target. "He's inside the diamond!" he yelled.

"Good shot, Davy!" Pa said with a smile. "Only Jason got nearer the center."

Davy was content. His world had been shattered and then rebuilt. There wasn't anything that he could say, but at supper that night he was very hungry.

Davy Begins to Hunt

THE CROCKETTS went to live on Cove Creek early the next spring. The new house was not finished when the family arrived. It was not the usual two-room cabin with loft above. It had two full stories and the rooms were large. The lower rooms still had only dirt floors, but Mr. Crockett proudly said there would be solid wooden floors by winter. He even talked grandly of having window glass brought over the mountains. Until that was possible, wooden shutters would have to do, he said.

The house was a gristmill as well as a place to live. Cove Creek ran only a few feet from the house. A short flume would bring water to flow over a huge wooden wheel that would almost cover one end of the house.

Davy had visited mills with his father. He knew that no one was so important as a miller. He was eager for the mill to be in operation.

However, it took days and days of work to make the great wheel, to build the flume, to finish the house. Men from neighboring clearings came to help. Tom Galbraith, who would help run the mill, moved in with the family. He had furnished the millstones.

Davy soon tired of the building. The men who came to help with the work brought their rifles along. Davy examined them all.

One man said, "I never did see a boy love a gun so much."

Another said, "He's close kin to a snapping turtle. He needs a rifle for each hand."

"Somebody had better tell the bears to be on

the move. When Davy gets started, he'll really move fast."

All the men laughed, but Davy paid no attention. He could not stay away from the rifles.

Mr. Crockett said, "Davy, you must not handle the men's rifles."

Davy tried hard not to. He would sit on the ground and gaze at the long barrels. They were kept shiny with oil rags. He would look at the flintlocks and the hammers. He studied the brass plates set into the stocks.

Sooner or later he had to put his hands on the stock, just to feel the polished wood. He would touch the flint and the hammer and lock gently and lovingly.

Sometimes a rifle would be left lying on a log, or even on the dry ground. Lying prone, Davy would stretch out behind the rifle. He would sight along the barrel till he fixed the brass bead clearly against some object. Then his forefinger would squeeze an imaginary trigger as he "fired" at his target.

When Mr. Crockett caught him handling a rifle, he whipped him. He set Davy jobs to do far from where the rifles were left. Always Davy came back to them.

Finally Uncle Joe said, "Davy's not worth much here. Why not let him hunt?"

Mr. Crockett said, "He's not big enough to go into the forest by himself. Nobody has time to go hunting with him, and I have no money to buy bullets for him to waste."

"Pa!" exclaimed Davy. "I'm big enough. I hit inside the diamond at Christmas."

"On your second try, and a bit of luck at that." Pa was not interested. "A rifle's longer than you are. You couldn't carry it."

"I can too! Can't I, Uncle Joe? I carried your gun home once, didn't I?"

"You certainly did, boy," Uncle Joe said, "and

you did a good job, too. He's worth a try, John. Maybe he'll get some game."

Pa frowned and looked angry. Davy was afraid he had argued till Pa would whip him, but he couldn't stop. "Pa, let me try just once. Just one bullet, Pa."

Mr. Crockett gave in. "All right, one bullet," he said. "One bullet a day as long as you bring something in—and if you can't kill your game I reckon you'll have nothing to eat. Everybody has to work to get this mill going."

Carefully Davy oiled Little Nancy, Pa's second gun, the one he let the boys use. All day long he practiced aiming. He lay down and shifted the long barrel. He lined up object after object with the tiny notch and the bright bead on the tip of the barrel.

The next day he was ready to start out early. A cow horn holding a small quantity of powder hung from his belt. His one bullet was safe in a tiny rawhide bag which also hung from his belt. He carried the rifle over his shoulder.

Uncle Joe walked with him part way into the forest. "Take it easy, Davy. Don't waste your bullet trying to get a deer, and don't ever shoot at a bear. You have to have dogs and a good knife for that. Even then it isn't safe for one man to take on a bear." Away from the clearing Uncle Joe stopped. "Let me see you load your rifle, boy," he said.

Davy sat on the ground and held the heavy gun. Proudly he opened his powder horn and poured a measure of powder into the barrel.

"A bit more powder, lad. Use this pea for a shot." Uncle Joe handed him one. "Now tamp it in. Aim at the fork of that oak tree."

The object was high but Uncle Joe showed Davy how to steady his rifle against a slender young sapling.

The boy fired. Uncle Joe produced more

peas and had him try again several times. "That's pretty good," he said at last. "Remember, Davy, you have only one bullet, so be sure you are right. Then go ahead. Now try once more."

Davy was growing impatient. He was wasting time shooting peas at an oak tree!

Uncle Joe said, "I'd sure like a squirrel stew for supper. There's a hickory grove about a mile upstream. That should be a good spot. Good luck!"

Davy went on alone. He felt grand. He was a hunter and he would bring home meat for everyone in the family.

It was easy to find the wood but it was a long way to carry the heavy rifle. Davy was tired when he arrived and he sat down to rest. Everything seemed quiet. He could see and hear nothing except the light rustle of tiny leaves in the trees overhead.

In a little while there was more movement.

Some birds twittered and flew from tree to tree. Branches creaked. Suddenly Davy heard squirrels chattering above his head. Looking up he saw not one squirrel but three, each sitting on a different limb.

And his rifle was not loaded.

Hastily Davy opened his powder horn, but in his haste he made too much noise. The squirrels scampered away and disappeared.

Grimly Davy loaded his rifle. He found a good spot to steady it and settled himself to watch. Now let those squirrels chatter at him!

He waited and waited. He sat so still that his legs went to sleep, but not one squirrel did he hear.

Walking about a bit, Davy studied the trees closely. He spotted a squirrel hole high on the trunk of a big hickory. The ground here was clear. He would have to brace the rifle barrel against a tree trunk.

Davy kept a close watch on the hole for a long time. Not a squirrel appeared. Finally he grew tired of standing and sank down on the mossy roots of an old tree. He could not see the hole so well now.

There was a noisy rustling of leaves off to the right. Davy rose to look but could see nothing. As he stared into the wood, a squirrel chattered and jeered on a limb above him. Davy was caught off guard but he swung the rifle into position. Not taking time to find a sufficient rest, he took quick sight and pulled the trigger.

A loud *cr-r-ac-ck* echoed among the great trees. The heavy gun kicked sharply against his shoulder and knocked the boy to the ground.

Davy hardly felt the blow. He had seen the squirrel tumble from the branch. He sat up and his eyes searched the ground. Not twenty feet away from him lay a dead squirrel. Davy jumped to his feet and ran to pick the squirrel up. There was a bullet hole right through its neck. The inquisitive little squirrel had leaned too far out on the limb.

That night Davy told his mother, "That old squirrel was mighty uppity. He just kept saying, 'Shoot! Shoot! Can't hit me! Can't hit me! Yanh! Yanh!' I just had to get him."

The Freshet

ALL THAT SPRING Davy lived in the woods. Occasionally his father, Jason, or Uncle Joe would go hunting with him. From them, and even more from his own close watching and listening, Davy learned to know the woods and how to track and catch the animals that lived in them.

He learned to track wildcats and coons and possums from the water holes. From nibbled leaves he could guess the size of deer. He could recognize the faint cluck of a wild turkey. He learned to walk as quietly as the Indians did.

Usually Davy's one bullet a day was successful. Often Davy brought in a squirrel or a coon.

He shot one young deer, too. Luckily Uncle Joe and Jason were with him that day to help carry it home.

One day in late spring Davy was going home empty-handed. He had tried for a deer and missed. A moist wind blew in his face as he walked noiselessly down a narrow path through the canebrake. The walls of cane here were thick and heavy.

Suddenly, at a slight curve in the path, Davy's heart almost stopped. Only a few yards in front of him appeared an enormous wildcat. The beast slowed down, its body became tense, and it looked about with yellow glittering eyes. It was as surprised as the boy. It hesitated, sniffing gently.

Davy was startled, but he was too good a woodsman to make unnecessary noise. The animal was still unsure, still sniffing. It gave ground slightly.

Davy's temper flared. He would not run down a walled lane with a wildcat at his heels. He had too much pride for that.

With a yell he raced at the animal. His gun, held at an angle across his body, hit the cane on both sides of the path. The heavy rattling of the cane and the boy's yells were too much for the wildcat. It turned and fled.

The next day it began to rain. Day and night it poured. Sometimes there was wind and the tall trees swayed and lashed. Water dripped from every leaf. The ground was so wet that it was spongy.

By now the mill was ready to operate. From the huge water wheel the strong trunk of a young hickory tree ran through an opening in the second story of the building to the upper millstone. The lower stone was in place in the floor downstairs.

The flume was complete. Any time now the

gate that held back the creek waters could be opened. Everything was ready to begin, but the rains made the creek too strong and swift.

"Looks like we're having a second flood," said Uncle Joe.

"Well, it can't rain forty days and forty nights this time," Pa answered.

"It's sure not missing it much," Tom Galbraith snapped.

Ma was worried. She said, "It may not be a flood, but if this keeps up we'll all wash down Cove Creek right smack into the river."

Jason was worried about the mill. "If the flume gate broke and the water in the creek hit the wheel, the wheel would spin right off its axle," he said.

Then came the hardest rain of all.

"It's raining jumping catfish," said Uncle Joe.

"It didn't hit Noah any harder," said Tom Galbraith gloomily.

"I reckon that flume gate will hold. If it doesn't——" Jason shook his head. "Cove Creek's out of its banks now. If it rises much higher it will be in the house."

Ma was afraid. "I knew no house should be this close to a creek. We'll all be drowned right here."

The family might talk all they wanted to, but Mr. Crockett wasn't worried. "This is a good creek for a mill," he said. "Tom Galbraith and I picked it out before he bought the millstones in Pennsylvania and brought them over the mountains. This little freshet isn't anything."

Davy wasn't afraid either. He sat on a stool in front of the fire and listened to the wood crackle. Drops of water came down the flue and sizzled as they hit the flames.

Suddenly there was a new noise above the rushing roar of the creek.

"That's the flume gate giving way!" Jason

shouted. He jumped to his feet and started toward the door.

Pa ran after him.

The noise grew louder. A peculiar screeching filled the room. The house shook and swayed. The great wheel was straining to turn. Then the axle broke. The upper millstone dropped on the lower with a heavy thud, and the wheel whirled. It banged crazily against the wall until it fell with a loud crash and splash to the ground.

After the deafening noise the world seemed suddenly very quiet. There was only the rainfall, and the roar of the rushing waters in the creek.

All the Crocketts crowded to the door. Jason was the first one out. Then Pa sloshed into the mud, with Davy at his heels. The wind and the rain made the night too dark for them to see very much.

Pa turned back to the door. "All you young-sters stay in the house," he ordered. "You, Davy, get back out of the rain."

Jason came back to report. "It's gone, Pa. The wheel is smashed to pieces."

The boys wanted to talk, to ask questions, but Pa was in a black mood. "Keep quiet, Bill, Jim! All you young ones clear out to bed now. I reckon this house will stand tonight. Davy, shut up, I said!"

Polly had gone upstairs. She reported that there was a great hole in the end wall, but the rain and wind were from the opposite direc-tion. Nothing was really wet.

Pa was still shouting, "Get out of this room! Quick, all of you!"

Davy knew that his father was not angry at them but that he was worried. All the work to build the gristmill would have to be done over again now.

By morning the rain had stopped and the clouds were all gone, but the water in the creek still roared loudly.

When Davy woke, soon after sunrise, he lay listening. The sounds were different somehow. He jumped from his pallet bed and ran to the big opening in the wall.

The water was very high against the creek bluff opposite. By leaning out he could see the waterfall from the flume. That water splashed noisily into the overflow that covered all the low ground on the bank where the house stood. Under the swirling water he could see broken outlines of the wheel.

Jason's voice rang out suddenly. "Pa! Pa! We got a boat."

A boat! Davy dashed back to his pallet and grabbed the trousers and shirt he had dropped beside it when he got into bed.

The other boys were all awake, too. Everyone was dressing quickly and trying to get downstairs as fast as possible.

There was great confusion. Jason, Mr. Crockett, Mrs. Crockett, and Polly were calling to one another and to the boys. Davy understood nothing until he heard the word "guns." Little Nancy was resting on wall pegs in the lower room. Was she safe? He rushed for the stairs.

Water was knee deep in the house.

Jason and Tom Galbraith had a big heavy boat down the creek. They couldn't get it nearer the house.

Ma, holding little Sarah, had waded to the boat and climbed in. Davy could hear her calling. "Polly! Bring along the pewter bowls and the shears!"

Pa was still in the lower room. "Straight to the boat, boys!" he called. He picked up Joe and swung him to his shoulder. "Hold on to me, Janie. Come on, boys, let's go!"

94

Davy scrambled down the narrow steps, feeling for a firm footing. His eyes were fastened on the long hunting rifles, which still rested on the wall pegs.

As he got to the last step he started forward quickly. He slipped and almost fell into the cold water.

Pa shouted at him for being so clumsy. Bill steadied him on his feet and turned him toward the door, but Davy pulled away. Swiftly he made his way to the side wall. He stood on tiptoe, bracing himself against the wall, and lifted Little Nancy from her pegs.

He turned quickly for the door, but not two steps from the wall his feet slipped. There was a great splash as he sat down suddenly.

Pa turned to shout at him again, but his angry words turned into a laugh. "Good boy, Davy!"

The lad's head and shoulders were above water. They were wet from the splashing, but

Little Nancy was held high. Not even the wooden stock had more than a few drops of water on it.

"Hold it, son!" Pa stood Joe on a big chest and came back to take the rifle. Holding it in one hand, he gripped Davy's arm and gave him a boost up.

"You help Janie to the boat," said Pa. "I'll bring the guns. They're all we have left."

The boat, with the whole Crockett family, was heavily loaded. Tom Galbraith helped Jason with the poling. Half poling, half rowing, the men brought the boat slowly along the edge of the current.

A half mile downstream there was a small creek. On the bank stood a deserted log cabin. Here the Crocketts took shelter.

The Tavern

THE HIGH WATER in Cove Creek lasted only a few days. The Crocketts could not move back into their house, however. The dirt floors dried out slowly.

They had to stay in the tumble-down hut. It had a floor of puncheon logs, but the roof sagged. There were open chinks in the mud plaster between the rotting logs. Luckily there was no more rain and the late spring days were turning warm.

The powder had got wet in the flood, as had much of the stored food. Davy was not allowed even one bullet a day for hunting.

Everyone was cross and unhappy. Pa never wanted to tell stories. He answered angrily when he was spoken to. After a meal of scorched bread and jerked venison, he would sit on a stump near the creek. Sometimes he would whittle. Sometimes he would just sit and stare into space.

Davy longed for the old days when Pa was always ready to talk. "Pa, tell me about fighting the Britishers. About the time you and Uncle John——"

"Don't you 'Uncle John' me or I'll whip you within an inch of your life," Pa said angrily. He got up and slouched toward the trail, and Davy turned away unhappily. Poor Pa! He was taking the loss of the mill hard.

Ma blamed Tom Galbraith for talking Mr. Crockett into building a mill. "That Tom hangs around like a hound."

Polly defended him. "Milling is good work,

Ma. It's steady. Tom bought those millstones with money he made trapping. Pa didn't pay a copper penny."

"Your pa didn't clear ground and plant corn either. I don't know where we'll get food to eat this year. That Tom! Why didn't he stay in the woods with his traps?"

Tom moved the millstones from the house on Cove Creek. He built a small mill on Little Sinking Creek. Soon Polly married him and went there to live.

Suddenly Jason announced that he was leaving. He went to live with the Bean family on the Holston River. Mr. Bean made the best rifles in all the valley. Jason wanted to learn to make rifles, to work with iron.

Wilson was gone, too. He went to Jonesboro, Tennessee, to visit his Uncle Robert Crockett.

Davy moped about the woods. He couldn't hunt with a slingshot. Indians killed game with bows and arrows, he knew, but he had never used them. Anyway, he was a rifle hunter. He didn't want a toy.

One day in early September Davy and Bill went up Cove Creek to a big pool to fish. They took spears of white-oak sticks which they had whittled in Indian fashion. Luck was good that day. They strung eleven nice mountain trout on a grapevine and started home.

Pa was coming up the main trail as they approached the cabin. He was singing happily:

> "Over the river to feed my sheep
> And over the river to Charley,
> Over the river to feed my sheep
> On buckwheat cakes and barley."

Then he saw the boys. "Hey, William! Davy! We're moving. We're leaving this hut here in the woods. We're going to move to the main trail!"

100

Ma came through the sagging door to see what was going on.

"Get ready, Rebecca. We're not living in this water trap another day."

Ma didn't know whether to be pleased or not. Pa had been excited over moving so many times before. "Where are you taking us this time, John Crockett?"

"We're moving to the main trail. We'll live out where people come and go and stop. Yes, sir, we will be right where they stop. We're going to have a tavern!"

"A tavern, Pa?" the boys cried together.

"Yes-siree and a bobtail! A tavern where folks will stop to spend the night and people will come in to eat and drink. They'll sit around and talk, and you'll hear all about politics and what is going on in the big world, Bill. Davy, you'll hear the biggest liars in all creation tell their yarns."

"Not a tavern, John!" Ma objected. "We don't

know a thing about running a tavern. We haven't any money to buy one. It would be an awful amount of work."

"Now, Becky, don't you worry. I've got the tavern. Sure it will be work, but good honest work never hurt——"

Davy broke in. "Can I hunt there, Pa?"

"Sure, boy. Just as fast as we can make enough money to buy lead for bullets. It's fine hunting country."

"What are you going to do to make money, John Crockett? Answer me that." Ma was changing the subject, Davy thought.

Pa paid no attention to the question. "Now, Ma, you'll like this place. It's right on the main road. Folks will be going down to Knoxville, and they'll stop and spend the night with us. Then they'll be traveling from Knoxville back up to Abingdon in Virginia. Oh, there are lots of people traveling through the mountains these days—fine folks going out to see the great new country west of us. We will be right there on the road, and they'll sleep the night and eat a meal with us and change their horses. It will be a grand life, Becky."

"What about clear land, John? Aren't you going to plant?"

"Sure, sure, Becky. There's a bit of clearing. But mainly we'll all be busy in the tavern. The boys can take care of the horses. Janie can help get meals till we make enough money to get some servants. Rebecca, it's the greatest chance yet. Why, it's lucky that freshet washed out the mill. We'd never see people or make money either on old Cove Creek."

The tavern did not live up to Mr. Crockett's fine words, however. It was a poor place. Only poor men stopped there: wagoners who hauled supplies over the new post road from Virginia and Pennsylvania down to Knoxville; cattle

drovers driving herds up the valley to markets in the cities. The folk who rode fine horses and traveled in carriages went right by to seek larger inns.

Davy didn't like the tavern. He didn't like to carry piggins of water for work horses. He didn't like to stay awake at night herding cattle around a fire. He didn't like having to serve other people, either.

Only the taproom was sometimes fun. Mr. Crockett stayed there, talking, handing out the food and drink, telling and hearing tales.

Davy loved the tales told. He had already learned there were two kinds of stories. Either kind could be exciting; either kind could be funny, too.

One kind was true. The other kind was entertaining, and a boy believed only as much of it as he wished. Davy liked the true stories, which were mostly about Indians and fighting, but he liked the other kind of a story better—the kind that wasn't really true.

"Plenty Christians hereabout now," a man said one night. "When I first came here in 1773, though, there was not much but Indians. They were always getting in the way, roaming about the country hunting and spying—and getting into things!

"One year I had a fine crop of red clover hay. I cut it all careful and piled it into cocks. I hung my scythe up in a hickory tree while I went off to get my oxen to haul in the hay.

"Then one of my hounds started growling. I looked back and there were four—five—ten Indians gathering up those cocks as fast as they could. I grabbed up my rifle and killed one Indian right off. Then I picked off a couple more. They were bent on stealing that hay. I rushed right at them, a-swinging my scythe.

"I must have killed a dozen of the scalawags.

The ground was plumb wet with Indian blood, wherever you looked.

"Do you know, the next year I got a double crop! About as much Indian grass came up as clover, though. Every tuft of it was stiff and sharp like an Indian scalp lock. The clover was all copper-red, too."

The men sitting around the room laughed.

"Can't beat Sam on a tale," one said.

Davy grinned, too. He was delighted by the silly ending.

"Look at young Davy grin," someone said.

"He grins just like a coon," said another.

"No, he's a better grinner than a coon. Aren't you, Davy?"

"Say, Davy, ever try outgrinning a coon? I'd bet on you."

Teasing made Davy angry. Sometimes he answered hotly. Sometimes he sulked. He wished he were big enough to fight these grown men. Once in a while he did try to pick a fight with them.

"Leave the boy alone, men," his father would say. "He's quirky."

"Sure, he's half alligator, half horse, and a little touched with snapping. turtle. I bet his cradle was a snapping turtle's shell."

Davy's mother said, "Make them laugh and they'll quit teasing you, Davy. Tell them a story. Tell them how you can outgrin a coon."

Davy tried. Soon he had a good story for anyone who tried to tease him.

"Everybody around here keeps saying I can outgrin a coon," Davy told the men around the fire one night. "Well, I finally decided I'd just try my luck. So I've been practicing every time I've run across one of those varmints out in the woods."

"What luck have you had, Davy?" one man wanted to know, grinning.

"I've had right good luck off and on," the boy said. "Sometimes, of course, I can't get the coon to look me in the eye. Then he won't try to beat me in a grin. But just let him really get a good look at my grin and he'll set himself to outdo me."

"What happens then?"

"The coon stands it as long as he can and then he tumbles right off that limb and we have coon for supper."

"Wow! That's sure all we've had to eat around here this week. Davy, I'll say you must be a real hunter!"

"Yes, sir, but last night I didn't have any luck. I was walking down the trail and I saw as likely a coon as you'd ever hope to see on a big limb. I sat down and started to grin. I grinned and I grinned. That coon just stayed right in the same spot and never moved.

"Well, I propped my head up on the hickory

stick I was carrying and went on grinning. After a good while I got tired. I decided I'd climb the tree to see why that coon was so determined to stay. Up I went. And do you know what I found?"

"A dead coon!" one man shouted.

"No, sir. It was a big knot on the limb."

Everyone laughed.

Davy went on: "But that's not all. My grin had shucked every bit of bark off that knot. It was as smooth and bald as Uncle Nate's head."

Davy's Trip

On August 17, 1798, Davy Crockett was twelve years old. He was a tall, slender, black-haired, red-cheeked boy.

He had never been to school a day in his life. There was no school within miles of his home. There wasn't even a book in his father's house. John Crocket had once had some, but the Crocketts had moved often and gradually the books had been lost. Davy hardly remembered what one looked like.

Wilson did. He had come home from Jonesboro. During the months he had lived with Uncle Robert he had gone to school and learned to read. Uncle Robert had books. He had newspapers, too, and Wilson had liked to read about things that were happening. There was news of Congress, of Philadelphia and New York, of George Washington and Thomas Jefferson. There was news also of Tennessee. It had been recognized as a state for a little more than two years.

Wilson was worried because Davy knew so little about books and the country.

Davy said, "I live on the Abingdon trail."

Wilson told him, "But, Davy, you live in Tennessee and Tennessee is one of the states in the Union."

Davy argued, "Aw, Tennessee's a river. Everybody knows that."

"Sure, it's a big river, but Tennessee's a state, too. It's the newest state in the Union. I can't name all the other fifteen."

Davy was not interested. "When I get big

I'm going to get a rifle and a canoe and I'm going down the Tennessee River where no one lives but Indians and I'm going to kill bears."

However, Davy's first trip was not to be down the Tennessee River into the wilderness after all. It was not even to be an adventure as Davy thought of adventure.

One night a Dutchman named Jacob Siler stopped at the tavern. His wife was sick and he was moving from Tennessee back to Virginia where her father lived. Mr. Siler had a drove of cattle.

"Mr. Crockett," he suggested, "I can't take care of my family and see after these cows, too. If you'll send one of your boys with me I'll pay him good wages."

Things were going badly at the tavern. Mr. Crockett was always glad to make some extra money. Jim was already hired out to a farmer in the neighborhood.

"That'll be fine, Jacob," Pa said. "Wilson! You go tell your ma you're going to drive cattle for Mr. Siler."

"Oh, but, Pa!" Wilson objected. "Mr Kitchen is opening his school next week and you promised me——"

"Pa, let me go," Davy begged.

Mr. Siler agreed to take Davy. Mr. Crockett warned him. "He's a good boy, Jacob, but he's quirky. His temper flies off the handle mighty easy, but it's on again quick, too."

Davy felt big. He had a job and he was going off to Virginia. He was cocky as he went about his work that night. He herded the cows to the branch for water. He circled the drove as it bedded down for the night.

After supper he took down the long rifle from its pegs on the cookroom walls. "Reckon I'd better get Nancy in good shape for traveling," he said boastfully.

114

At first Mr. Crockett did not notice what Davy was doing. Suddenly, in the midst of his work, Davy felt a hand on his shoulder.

"It's time you were in bed, boy," said Mr. Crockett. "You know, Jacob wants to be on his way at daybreak."

"Yes, sir, Pa. Look how Little Nancy shines. She's as clean as new snow on a pine tree."

Pa grinned. "Good boy, Davy," he said, "but I'll have no time to hunt, with Wilson in school and you gone."

Davy did not understand. "I expect there'll be bears in Virginia, Pa, and we'll be on the old Indian trail——"

Mr. Siler spoke up then. "That boy carries no rifle, John Crockett. He'll kill a cow with it sure as thunder."

Pa agreed. "This is no hunting trip, Davy. You'll be driving cattle. Get to bed now." He patted Davy's shoulder and gave him a shove.

Davy pulled away from his father. He put the rifle back on its peg in the kitchen and then climbed the ladder to the loft above. He was too angry to speak.

He stretched out stiffly on the pine-needle and bearskin bedding. It was early autumn and the night outside was cool, but in the little attic room it was warm and stuffy. A tiny breath of air came through the open shutter. A single star winked solemnly at the boy.

What, Davy wondered, did a man do on a mountain trail without a rifle? Of course he wouldn't shoot a cow, not one of those mooing brutes! He wasn't a silly child; he was a hunter. But what would he do if a wildcat or a wolf or a bear tried to steal a cow?

He got up from his pallet and felt along the wall till he found the tomahawk Jason had sent him for his birthday. He lifted the thong from the peg and drew the sharp blade from its

116

leather sheath. He balanced the weapon in his hand. Then he took a throwing grip.

He stepped back in the darkness and took aim at the wooden shutter. He estimated the distance, shifted his aim slightly and threw. The tomahawk hit the shutter low and clattered to the floor.

"Guess I'll have to practice a lot," Davy thought. Still, he felt a little better when he went back to bed.

The early morning start was not so bad. Davy was the center of attention. Janie had a big packet of food ready for him. Ma had stuffed clothes into a knapsack. On top was a warm fur rug to roll around him at night. Little Joe was jealous. Even Wilson was almost sorry he had chosen to go to school rather than set out on adventure.

Mrs. Siler climbed into the creaking wagon with her two small children. It was loaded high with the stove, the loom and the spinning wheel, the plow and the tools which the Silers had brought when they came into the wilderness to make their home. Now they were going "back yonder" to a more settled community, to relatives, to a church and stores.

"Step smartly now, lad, and mind you do what Mr. Siler tells you," Pa said as he clapped Davy on the back.

Ma gave Davy a rough hug. "Be a good boy," she said. "Don't forget you're the lad who can outgrin a coon." She smiled broadly.

Davy grinned back and walked off with a swagger. Mr. Siler yelled. His two shepherd dogs, Hans and Gretel, barked. The noise started the cows moving, on the trail northward. Importantly, Davy added his shouts.

Where a big blazed oak marked the bend of the trail, Davy turned to wave. Ma and Janie were still standing in the yard. Pa was standing in the doorway, watching. He raised one hand when Davy turned.

Davy tried to grin, but his lips puckered instead. A sad whistle came out. He tried a second time. The older dog gravely continued to circle the cows, but lively Gretel answered the whistle. Davy had a new friend.

The trail led north, veering slightly west. Much of the way was a clear path through the woods. For many years it had been the main warpath of the Indian tribes who held the southern mountains.

The Indians had followed animal trails to the best places to ford the streams and rivers. The path curved around hills and small mountains. It avoided steep climbs whenever possible.

Of late many travelers, on horseback, on foot, in wagons or in high-wheeled carriages, had traveled on the Wilderness Road. It was a slow, roundabout route, but as long as one kept to the

main trail there was little danger of getting lost
along the way.

Mr. Siler walked in front, carrying a hickory
stick with a heavy leather lash. His rifle was held
in special slots high on the side of the wagon.
Always the stocky Dutchman kept a keen eye

120

open for places in the wood into which the cattle might accidentally stray.

Much of the time Mrs. Siler rode, with the baby on her lap. The little girl perched on the jolting seat beside her. Sometimes Mrs. Siler would leave the children asleep and walk beside her husband for a while.

Neither Mr. Siler nor his wife talked much. Occasionally one or both sang songs in a language Davy couldn't understand. The children were both tiny. Except for Gretel, Davy felt that he had no friend. The trail to Virginia was long and slow and the boy was lonely.

Following the slow-moving cows, or guarding them when Mr. Siler stopped to let them graze, Davy practiced throwing his tomahawk. He would sight an imaginary wildcat in a small tree. He would stalk closer and hurl the weapon. "Got you! Right between the eyes," he would praise himself as he drew the blade from the wood. Or if he missed he would say, "Got away, did you, you varmint? You'll lick that wound for a long time."

Mr. Siler grumbled. "You be careful, boy. You kill a fine cow someday." However, he didn't take Davy's tomahawk away, and Davy continued to practice whenever he could.

One night as they made camp, Davy said to Mr. Siler, "A boy at the last tavern told me there were fine turkeys on this ridge. If we camped here tomorrow I bet I could shoot one of them."

Mr. Siler just grunted, "Nanh, nanh."

Later Davy lay on his back, looking up at the stars. With a split cane he had whittled into a whistle, he tried to make soft turkey calls, but without much luck.

"It's no good, boy," Mr. Siler said suddenly. "You too little to hunt turkey. You drive cows. Maybe in Virginia you hunt rabbits."

Davy blushed angrily at being called "too little," but Mr. Siler paid no more attention to him.
Davy continued to practice.

Many days up the trail they turned away from
the well-traveled Wilderness Road and headed
east. One night they camped in a deserted clearing, where someone had once had a cabin.

Mrs. Siler went over to some old apple trees
to gather fruit. When her apron was full, she
called to Davy to bring her a small pail.

Davy got the pail and hurried over to help
her. He was almost at her side when he heard a
clear *"Br-r-rr—br-rr-r-rr."*

He dropped the pail and jerked his tomahawk
from the sheath on his belt.

In an instant he spotted the rattlesnake. It
was within two feet of Mrs. Siler, coiled and
ready to strike. Davy aimed quickly and threw.
The blade of his tomahawk pinned the snake to
the ground.

Mrs. Siler looked at the snake and shivered. Then she said, "Thank you, Davy. That was quick thinking. I didn't even see that snake."

Mr. Siler said nothing. He just looked at the snake and turned it over with the toe of his boot, then walked away. That evening, however, when he went to check the cattle, Davy passed close to Mr. Siler beside the campfire. Without a word Mr. Siler reached up and clapped him awkwardly on the shoulder.

Davy was proud of the five rattles from the snake's tail and put them on his cap. Whenever he moved or shook his head they rattled drily.

The Silers' baby liked the rattles, too. He liked to watch them and to listen to them when Davy stopped to play with him. He would gurgle and wave his hands every time he saw Davy.

"See him," Davy said to Mrs. Siler one day. "See him listen to the rattles. He likes to hear them. Watch."

124

Davy shook his head and the baby laughed aloud. Davy and Mrs. Siler laughed, too.

Finally Davy took the rattles from his cap and gave them to the baby. He hated to give them up. He had wanted to take them home and show them to Pa and the rest of the family, but they would please the baby more.

In Virginia

THE LAST FEW days of the journey were disagreeable. The wind was cold and there were flurries of rain. Mr. Siler made the cattle travel faster. He wanted to get home.

There were many clearings now. The fields were large and sometimes they were fenced. Many of the houses were of stone or brick.

Davy was tired and footsore. Even worse, he was lonesome and homesick. He wanted talk and laughter. Mr. Siler was a stern master. "No loitering around the taproom," he had ordered each night his party had stopped at a tavern. "We leave early in the morning."

The Dutchman made no threats and he did not whip Davy. The boy was afraid not to obey him. It was very different treatment from John Crockett's quick roughness and hearty laughter.

Mrs. Siler's father was named Mr. Hartley. Davy was glad to reach his farm near Rock Bridge. The house was large and there were many cleared fields around it.

There were several boys in the Hartley family. One of them, named Jake, was only a little older than Davy.

Davy had thought he would start back to Tennessee immediately. He was surprised when Mr. Siler said, "You good boy, Davy. I pay you for work. You stay with me."

He handed Davy six big round silver dollars. The boy had never held so much money in his hand before.

"Thank you, sir," he said, "but I must get home. Pa needs me in the tavern."

"No, you stay with me, Davy. I get farm soon. You help with cattle."

Pa had said, "Do what Mr. Siler says, Davy." The boy didn't know what to do. He didn't like the cleared fields of Virginia. He didn't feel at home in the Dutch farm family.

He wanted to get back to the great forested valleys on the other side of the mountains. He wanted to hear the laughter and songs and talk in his father's tavern.

Like the woodsmen, he loved the tales of Tennessee heroes like Daniel Boone and Bigfoot Spencer and John Sevier. He loved the stories traders had learned from Indians about animals who talked and acted like human beings. He loved the ridiculous lies that men told solemnly when they took part in "tall talk."

Above all Davy wanted to hunt. He had six silver dollars. He could buy enough lead and powder to last forever with them. Maybe he even had enough to buy a rifle. If he had his own rifle, he could hunt whenever he wished.

The big problem, though, was how to get back home. Mr. Siler said, "Stay." Maybe Pa had given him to Mr. Siler, Davy thought. Maybe he had to stay here and work as long as Mr. Siler wanted him to.

The Hartley boys did not talk much, but they loved to hear Davy's tall tales. "Tell us how you outgrinned a coon, Davy," one would say.

"Davy, how big was the biggest bear you ever saw?" another would ask.

"Aren't you scared of wildcats when you're in the woods, Davy?" another asked.

Davy remembered the wildcat in the cane-brake and decided to give the boys some tall talk.

"Well," he said slowly, making up his story as he went along, "I'm not rightly afraid of a wild-cat unless it's really mad. I tamed a wildcat once back home."

"A little baby cat?" Jake asked. "I bet he was cute, wasn't he?"

"No," Davy answered with a serious face. "This was a full-grown wildcat. It was this way. I was coming home from a hunting trip one day with a deer I had just shot slung over one shoulder. When I got to the creek I put down the deer to get a drink. I turned around and there was Mr. Wildcat just ready to spring for my deer.

"I threw it across the creek so the cat couldn't get it. Then I said, 'That's my meat and you can't take it away from me.'

"The cat bared his teeth and snarled at me. I showed my teeth and growled at him. He shook his head and stamped on the ground. I flapped my arms and kicked my heels together. We circled around a bit, growling and grinning and making faces. Then he started toward me. I landed a blow right on his nose. He bellowed

130

and swiped at me with a big claw. I stepped away real fast, but his claw raked my arm just the same.

"That made me mad, and I tore into him good and proper. I was a regular whirlwind. I hit him on the nose and then I jumped on his back and bit his ear. I just generally raised such a dust he couldn't find where I was.

"Finally that old cat lay down on the ground. He put his paws over his eyes and whimpered. So I stopped pounding him. I put my foot on his head. 'You're my cat,' I said. I took him home with me and he does all my chores."

"What can he do?" demanded Jake.

"Why," said Davy grandly, "he can put wood on the fire, and he rakes the garden to plant seeds in the spring, and when I get real cold he does my shivering for me."

At that the boys all laughed. They knew then that Davy was just making up a big tale.

Even though he enjoyed the Hartley boys, Davy was still lonesome and wanted to go home. One afternoon he wandered off by himself to a wooded section of the farm. There were few signs of animals, but that didn't matter. He didn't have a gun anyway.

On the edge of a field he stopped to look out across the country. He did not realize that his ears were sorting out the wind noises and bird calls around him. Suddenly he listened closely.

He heard clear, harsh tones that seemed to say, "*Crk-crk-ket-kt, cr-crket-t.*"

He looked around to see what made the sounds. Then he saw a flock of black-and-brown speckled guineas feeding in the field. Davy laughed and walked home with a swagger.

"I guess I must be somebody even way up here in Virginia," he said. "Even the birds know my name."

He practiced making the guinea call, clicking his tongue against his teeth: *"Crk-crk-kett—Cr-crk-k-k-tt."*

It sounded like the guinea hens talking, but it said his name, just as plainly as could be.

Davy helped with the early winter work about the farm, but he wasn't happy. He kept wanting to hunt. He imagined sighting down the long barrel of a rifle, lining up the shining bead tip and his game. He wanted to hear the thin, high *crack* of the exploding powder sending the bullet from the barrel. He wanted to feel the heavy thud of a rifle against his shoulder.

It was too late now to hunt a turkey gobbler. The ducks and high-flying geese had gone far to the south. Soon even the bears would be bedded down in hollow trees to sleep through the cold winter. However, there were still wolves and foxes and deer.

One day Davy was playing with the Hartley boys near the road that led to the Wilderness

Road. Some wagons came by, and the boys called greetings to the drivers.

Davy recognized one of them. His name was Dunn, and he had spent several nights at Crockett's Tavern. He made his living hauling corn, flax, furs, and other produce from the wilderness to the towns of Virginia. On his return trips he loaded his wagon with cloth, boxes of spices, iron bars, and barrels of flour.

Davy left the boys to run toward Mr. Dunn's wagon. "Hey, Mr. Dunn!" he yelled.

Mr. Dunn looked at him without recognition.

"I'm Davy Crockett, and I live on the Abingdon trail," Davy said.

Mr. Dunn spat over the high wheel and pulled his horses to a stop. "Well, are you now? John Crockett's youngster. Say, you're the boy that outgrins a coon!" The man slapped his thigh and laughed. "What are you doing way off up here in Virginny?"

134

Davy climbed on the wagon and perched on a pile of boxes. "Let me ride a little way, Mr. Dunn," he said.

The man clucked to his horses and they moved on at their slow, even pace.

"I drove some cattle up here with a man this fall and he wants me to stay with him. He wants me to farm."

"Well, that's a fine life, boy."

"I don't like it," Davy said. "I don't want to be a farmer. I'm a hunter."

Mr. Dunn laughed at Davy's boastfulness. He spat again and slapped the reins over the horses' back. "Isn't he good to you, Davy?"

"Yes, sir. He treats me all right, and he paid me good wages. Mr. Dunn," the boy continued earnestly, "he paid me in silver dollars. I could pay you if you'd let me ride home with you in your wagon."

Mr. Dunn pulled the reins to halt the horses.

"Whoa!" he said. He sat back and looked back at Davy. Once or twice he started to speak. His brow furrowed as he studied the problem. Finally he asked, "What did your pa tell you when you left home?"

"He told me to mind Mr. Siler, and I have, but he didn't say how long I should stay. Mr. Dunn, I want to go home awfully bad."

"What does Siler say?"

"He just grunts and says, 'Nyah, nyah, boy. You too little to start off to Tennessee.'"

Mr. Dunn laughed again. The other wagons had gone on ahead. He studied the sky. "Well, Davy," he said. "I reckon if Siler paid you the money you must be a free boy. He'd have paid your pa if you were apprenticed out to work."

Davy said nothing. Mr. Dunn gathered up the reins again. "The boys and I are stopping at Tyler's Tavern down the road tonight. Know where it is?"

"Yes, sir. I've been there."

"Well, you be there by daylight tomorrow if you want to travel with us. There's snow in that sky and we've got to push along fast."

Davy jumped to the ground. "I'll be there."

The man clucked to his horses and Davy raced back to the farm. He was excited, but he couldn't tell the boys. They might tell Mr. Siler, and Mr. Siler wouldn't let him go.

It was Sunday afternoon and the family had gone visiting. The boys had been left at home to do the night chores. Davy did his share hurriedly. While the other boys were still in the barn, he went upstairs. He put all his clothes into the bag his mother had given him. He left it between his low bed and the wall. He hoped the boys would not notice it. His six precious dollars he tied tightly in a small leather pouch.

After supper he went to bed early. None of the Hartley boys noticed anything unusual.

138

Davy tried hard to sleep, but he kept waking up. It was hard to lie still. It was a dark night and he could see no star to give him an idea what time it was. Finally Davy could stand it no longer. It must be time for him to start. He had seven miles to walk before daybreak.

It would be easier, he decided, to go down the stairs and out the kitchen door. One of the Hartley boys slept in the kitchen. He snored so loudly, however, that no one would hear Davy open the door.

Davy crept slowly down the stairs and through the sleeping house. Only a little light flickered from the banked fires downstairs.

Several times his foot or his bag hit something. Davy stopped and held his breath. Finally he stood in the cold air with the door closed behind him.

He took a deep breath and moved forward. As he turned the corner of the house he got a surprise. Big snowflakes hit his face softly and moistly. The sky was black.

The tiny, flickering flames from inside the house made enough light to show him which way the road lay. A few yards from the house he was swallowed up in darkness. The half mile across the fields to the road was slow going.

Luckily the snow had just begun. Davy could feel the stubble or grass or dirt under his feet, but he could barely see the trees.

Finally the boy reached the road. Here the way was a narrow open strip between trees. The sky above was only slightly less black than the ground, but it was light enough to show him the rough road.

The snow was falling faster now. Davy made slow progress, but he didn't stop. Sometimes he slipped and fell, but he kept on the road and kept going.

When he reached the tavern men were up and

fires were burning brightly. One man called.

"Here's your lad, Dunn. I didn't believe he could make it."

"Sure he made it," Mr. Dunn said. "I've seen Davy many times at Crockett's Tavern. He's the boy who is kin to a snapping turtle. He won't let go till it thunders."

Davy grinned at him. "My Uncle Joe says, 'Be sure your're right and then go ahead.' That's my motto, too."

He edged up to the fire. It was good to get warm, to smell a hot breakfast cooking, to be with friends from Tennessee. Best of all, it was good to be going home.

Davy's Rifle

Davy's father had found the right occupation when he became a tavernkeeper. He still did a little farming, and he raised a few cows and horses to sell to traders going through the country, but often he lost money on his trades. He was not a good businessman.

Mr. Crockett remained a poor man. His tavern continued to be an inn for poor travelers, but hunters liked to gather there, too. They would sit by the big fireplace and tell tales of their adventures. They set up targets outside and had shooting contests.

To Davy, back from Virginia, the talk and

the shooting were both wonderful. He had lived with strangers; now he was home again.

There was much boasting and banter.

"I can outshoot, outrun, outfight, outswim any man in the country," one man would say.

"I can hit the string of a kite flying in a March wind," another would boast.

"You've watched the gray geese flying high overhead and wished you could hit one, haven't you? Well, I get me one 'most every year."

Zip Cochran told of being in the woods armed only with a hunting knife and a club when his dogs treed a bear. "I couldn't shoot and I couldn't cut down the tree. I picked up a flat rock and started pounding on the tree trunk. The bear thought I was using an ax. He crept to the end of a limb and let go. He was so fat that he hit the ground like a ball, and he bounced right over the heads of my dogs. That gave him a head start to another tree. The dogs treed him three times and each time he bounced away from them."

"How'd you get him, Zip?"

"I never did get him! The last time he bounced he was so close to the river he dived right in. There was a flatboat coming downstream. Everybody on board got so nervous the bear swam away in the excitement."

"Bears are smart."

"They sure are. I saw a bear swimming in the Tennessee River when I was hunting down in Indian territory. A boatload of Indians was catching up with him, but he just swam along paying no mind. When they got alongside he raised up one paw and turned the boat over slick as a whistle. Not an Indian could touch him with his knife."

"Did you get him?"

"Not then. I didn't want to tell the Indians where I was hiding."

Davy made a turkey call from the wing bone of a turkey. As he sat before the fire listening to the talk, he blew through it softly. Tupe Williams brought out his call and the two of them "talked" together.

Tupe said, "There was an old turkey gobbler I hunted three years. I knew his gobble as well as I know the voice of my dog when he's off baying through the woods. The gobbler knew me, too. He'd cluck right back at me, but he'd never get close enough for me to get a shot. He could find just where I was by spying on my boot marks. That was a smart old gobbler.

"One day I decided I had to have him. I thought up a way to do it. I put on my boots backward and walked up to a beech hollow that way. I gave just one call as if I was going away from there.

"That old gobbler answered right back. Then he ran around behind me to find my tracks. When he saw heel marks going down the ridge, he crowed a couple of times like a fighting cock. He was so sure I'd given up he came straight up to my hollow to feed on the beech mast. Mighty good eating he was, too. Never tasted better."

The winter that followed was long and cold. Davy chopped wood for the fires. He whittled a new hickory broom. He made moccasins from the hides of deer.

One day in the spring a traveler stopped at the tavern. He came by the stagecoach that made two round trips a week from Abingdon to Knoxville.

The young man was wearing a fine cloth suit and he brought a suit of hunting clothes, too. In a leather case he had the prettiest rifle Davy had ever seen.

It was not so long or heavy as those the frontiersmen used. The stock was polished walnut.

The barrel was a gleaming gray-black. The sighting notch and bead were made of silver. Davy studied it with admiration.

"My name is Martin," the stranger said to Mr. Crockett. "I've been told that I can get a guide here to show me real wilderness hunting. I'm not interested in ordinary deer or bear hunting. I'd like to shoot game in a section that has not been thoroughly hunted over."

Davy gazed in awe at the serious, superior young man. The hunters were all silent. No one looked at Mr. Martin directly. All of them were conscious of his city airs.

Mr. Crockett asked, "How long did you plan to hunt, Mr. Martin?"

"I'll have only a few days. The stagecoach was slow in reaching this place. I must return home shortly."

Zip Cochran spoke up. "I've been planning to go out Elk River way tomorrow or next day.

Mr. Martin may go along if he likes."

Mr. Martin asked if he would have real sport there. The hunters solemnly assured him it was wild country. They looked at Zip Cochran with admiring eyes.

A few years earlier a forest fire, started by lightning, had burned over a large area near Elk River. Little or no game had lived there since. There were no animal paths. The tall trunks of dead trees made it a ghostly region. Few hunters would dare to camp there.

Early in the afternoon, two days later, the hunters were back. Davy met them in front of the tavern.

"When does the next stagecoach go north?" Mr. Martin demanded.

"It leaves here about two hours before sundown," Davy told him.

Mr. Martin went into the tavern. Zip came up carrying both rifles. He handed one to Davy

and winked. "I doubt if Mr. Martin is very keen
on hunting, Davy," he said. "Maybe he'd sell
that rifle cheap."

Davy clutched the rifle. Swiftly he figured.
"I still have three dollars, but two bits have been

cut out of one. That's two dollars and six bits. If Pa would let me have some, I could pay him back in coonskins. I know I could!"

Small pieces of change were scarce in the backwoods. A silver dollar was sometimes cut into eight pieces and the bits used for change. One fourth of Davy's dollar had been cut away.

Boldly Davy walked into the tavern. "Pa," he said, "I could pay you back in coonskins if you would let me have some money to buy Mr. Martin's rifle."

"Do what, son? Buy a rifle?"

"Yes, sir. Mr. Martin doesn't like his rifle and I do. I've got three dollars but two bits were cut out of one."

"What does Mr. Martin want for his gun?"

"He didn't say, Pa, but it's cheap."

"Well, you'd better ask him."

Mr. Martin was sitting in an armchair, paying no attention to anyone. Davy went over to stand in front of him. For a moment Mr. Martin didn't even look up.

"I reckon this old rifle doesn't suit you much, does it, Mr. Martin? I reckon if you had a chance to sell it, you would, wouldn't you, sir?" he said eagerly.

Mr. Martin did not answer. He stared at the boy as though he did not realize he was there. Davy waited. "Mr. Martin, I'd give you five dollars and take this old rifle off your hands. I could pay Pa back in coonskins."

"Coonskins!" Mr. Martin's laugh was harsh. "Coonskins!" Then he looked directly at Davy. "What did you say, boy?"

"I'll give you five dollars for your rifle, sir," Davy repeated.

"Can you shoot a rifle?" Mr. Martin asked.

"Yes, sir. Sometimes I can hit a silver dollar at thirty yards." Davy wasn't boasting now. "I've shot a lot of squirrels and coons and possums, and one deer."

"Give me the money, boy," said the gentle-man. "You can use the gun better than I can."

That night the frontiersmen crowded around the old hunter. "What happened, Zip? Where's your game?"

"Gone on the stagecoach," Zip answered. "I saw he didn't know as much about how to handle a gun as a goose does about ribbed stockings. I didn't take chances. I took Mr. Martin out over Cat Brier Ridge. There's a right smart tangle of blackberries and cat briers and possum grapes in there. We hacked a way through till we got to a clear place under some dead hickory trees.

"By then it was almost night. At least it was so dark in all those vines it looked like night. I built up a big fire and we ate supper. Mr. Martin thought we should take turns sitting up to watch for wild beasts and I agreed. I took the first half. I got a good snooze, then I waked up and shook him to take his turn. He crawled out of his fur rug and grabbed up his rifle. I built up the fire some for him and lay back to watch.

"Way off I heard a panther scream. That boy sure did get scared. Then some owls flew over and hooted. I never did hear so many owls hooting together.

"Mr. Martin turned and twisted and looked out into the woods and moved nearer the fire. Once I saw him pour in powder and ram down a bullet. He made so much noise he'd have scared off anything but a bear. He spilled so much powder I was afraid the ground would catch on fire, too.

"He backed up against me, but I just snored as though I was sound asleep. Next morning he told me he'd spent the whole night scaring wildcats away. Said he saw their eyes, big as saucers. Maybe he did, but I guess it was just fox fire. I couldn't find any tracks. Anyway, he was white as hickory ash and I didn't have to ask him twice would he like to come in."

The hunters laughed heartily. This was the kind of joke they loved.

Davy hardly heard Zip's story. He was busy cleaning and polishing and testing his rifle. "Sally Ann's the finest rifle in Tennessee," he boasted to his brother Wilson.

Going to School

Sally Ann fitted Davy's height and arm better than any rifle he had ever used. The hunters soon gave him a chance to show what he could do with her.

One night they were having a shooting contest outside. Davy had set a smoky candle in the crotch of a tree. One after another, the men had aimed and shot at the little target. Only the best shots could hit the very tip of the wick, nipping off a bit of it but scarcely disturbing the flame.

"Not much breeze tonight, Davy," one man said. "I can snuff two candles to your one."

"Aw, Davy's got a city rifle," said another. "It can't do tricks."

"I'm betting on Davy," said a third. "He'll knock the candle clean over."

There was loud laughter.

"Naw," said Zip, "he'll come closer than that. He'll drill a hole an inch below the flame."

Davy said nothing. Sally Ann was on trial. He mustn't let her down. He heeded Zip's warning. If he didn't have his gun braced just right he was likely to shoot low.

A new candle was set up. It flared smokily in the light breeze. Davy stood behind the barrel rest, thirty yards away. He sighted carefully. His gun fitted his hand. The butt was snug against his shoulder.

He squeezed the trigger. The crack was loud in his ears. The candle flickered. The light jerked, then blazed brightly. The smoking tip of the wick had been neatly cut away

156

by the bullet. Davy straightened up, grinning broadly. Good old Sally Ann!

"Perfect shot!"

"Good boy, Davy!"

"Just luck. He can't do it again."

Davy patted his rifle. "I've got another bullet," he said.

Another candle was set up. Davy poured in powder and rammed home the bullet carefully. This time he stepped away from the barrel rest. Sally Ann was not so long as most rifles, but, even so, her barrel was long and heavy. It was hard work to hold her steady.

Davy pulled the trigger. Again the candle was snuffed. Its flame burned more brightly. The men cheered.

"Davy can outshoot, outrun, outeat, and outgrin anybody this side of the Mississippi River," Wilson boasted.

Wilson was proud of Davy's shooting, but he

thought his brother should know other things. Later that night the boys had an argument about the matter.

Wilson said, "Davy, you can't read or write. You should go to school."

Davy didn't care whether he could read or not. "Why should I learn to read?" he asked. "I'm going to be a hunter, and I can read animal signs. I'll never get lost in the woods. I know bear tracks, and I can tell what game a wildcat is tracking, and——"

"It's not the same thing, Davy. If you live all your life away in the woods and never see anybody, maybe it wouldn't matter, but you won't do that."

"Well, when I see people I can tell stories and sing and dance. I can beat them shooting, too," Davy ended boastfully.

Pa had not seemed to notice the boys' talk. Now he spoke suddenly, and sharply. "Davy, you'll go with Wilson and Joe when Mr. Kitchen opens his school again next week."

That was all. When Pa used that tone the boys didn't argue. Davy went to school.

Mr. Kitchen was a harsh schoolmaster. He kept hickory sticks on his desk. He whipped boys who did not know their lessons. He whipped them for not studying, for losing their slates, and for anything else he didn't like.

On the fourth day at school one of the big boys tripped Davy as he walked to the door. Davy didn't fall, but he bumped noisily into the front bench where the youngest students sat.

He turned on the boy who had tripped him. His quirky temper was hot. "You squash-headed, crow-eating piece of stump wood, you! Get up and fight!"

Mr. Kitchen caught Davy's arm. Davy got a whipping for causing a disturbance.

He slipped out of the schoolhouse a little

early. Down the road he stopped and waited. He was ready when the big bully came past. "Now I reckon you'll fight," he said. He rushed at the boy like a wildcat.

Davy won, and left the bully with a scratched, bruised face. Now what was he to do? Mr. Kitchen didn't approve of fighting. He would guess what had happened. Davy would get a harder whipping.

For several days Davy left home each morning with Wilson and Joe. He stayed in the woods all day. If he could have taken Sally Ann with him, he would have been happy.

"I'm not going back to that school," he decided. But what could he tell Pa?

Then Mr. Crockett found out. Mr. Kitchen asked him why Davy was not at school.

"He hasn't missed a day," declared Pa, "not even when Jesse Cheek wanted help to round up cattle to drive north."

161

"Davy hasn't been to school this week," said Mr. Kitchen.

Pa was angry when he saw Davy. "What's this about your missing school?"

Davy tried to explain. "Mr. Kitchen whipped me, sir. Then I had a fight with a boy and——"

"That's no good excuse. You'll get a worse whipping right here at home if you don't go."

Davy started for school, but now he was in a worse fix than ever. He was afraid to go to school. He was afraid to go home.

Then he remembered. His brother Bill was going with Mr. Cheek to take a big drove of cattle to Virginia. Maybe Mr. Cheek could use him, too.

Hard Knocks

THIS CATTLE DRIVE to Virginia was more fun than Davy's first trip. It was much longer. Mr. Cheek went past the town of Abingdon. He went on through the Valley of Virginia, through the towns of Lynchburg and Charlottesville, and on to Front Royal in the north.

There he sold his cattle and paid off the men. Most of them started home at once.

At first Davy was eager to get back home. He had missed Sally Ann. He thought of hunting in the woods. He thought of the men talking in the taproom and of his mother's good cooking. Then he remembered the whipping that

163

Pa had promised him, and his eagerness disappeared. He could do without that! Pa always meant what he said.

One night Davy heard a wagoner telling tales. He was a jolly fellow, who laughed a lot. His name was Adam Myers.

"You're a fine boy, Davy Crockett," Mr. Myers said. "Why don't you come along with me? I'm taking a wagonload of stuff to Gerardstown. We'll get a load there and head right back to Tennessee."

Bill spoke up. "I'm sorry, Mr. Myers, but Davy had better go along with us. Pa wouldn't like it if he didn't come home."

Davy remembered something else Pa didn't like. "I'll make just one trip with Mr. Myers," he said. "It won't be long till I'll be home. You tell Pa and Ma I will be right back."

"Yes-siree," said Mr. Myers. "I'm from Greenville and I've got a wife and children back there. I'm heading right back as soon as I make this trip."

"Davy, you didn't even take time to tell the folks good-by," Bill said. "Ma and Janie sure did miss you last time you drove cattle to Virginia. I know they're mighty unhappy now."

Davy shook his head. "Pa's worse than a turtle holding to a fisherman's toe when he gets mad," he said. "I'll give him a little more time to forget."

Davy was sorry to say good-by to Bill. He felt guilty at first, but Mr. Myers kept him laughing with his odd tales. The boy promised himself he would go home and take his medicine as quickly as Mr. Myers could reload.

Business was not good in Gerardstown. Mr. Myers went on to Alexandria to seek a load. Davy's money had run out, so he got a job as a farmer's plowboy at twenty-five cents a day.

He was ashamed now that he had run away

from home. It was too far to return alone. He worked hard and the farmer liked him. He stayed for several months. Mr. Myers continued to haul from Gerardstown to Alexandria or Baltimore. Davy saw him each time he came to Gerardstown.

By spring Davy had saved enough money to buy some good clothes. "I'd like to make a trip to Baltimore," he told Mr. Myers.

"It's a big city," said Mr. Myers, as they drove into town. "A country boy is likely to lose all his money here. If some fellow doesn't pick your pockets, the cheap merchants will trade you out of your eyeteeth."

"Maybe you'd better keep my money for me," Davy suggested. "If I find something I want to buy, I'll get it from you."

It was Adam Myers, not Davy, who lost or spent the money while they were in Baltimore. Perhaps he used it to buy the cargo with which they started back to Tennessee. Davy never knew, but his money was gone.

Not only that, something had happened to make Mr. Myers a changed man. He no longer laughed or told tales. He was bad-tempered now, and he threatened Davy with his wagon whip. He told Davy he had no money, but he would not tell the boy what he had done with it.

One morning before dawn Davy took his small bundle of clothes from the wagon and slipped away. He was miles from home, and he had not a cent of money, but he would not stay longer with a man he didn't trust.

There was nothing to do but go to work. Jobs were not easy to get. For a month Davy worked with a man who had a powder mill at Montgomery, in Virginia. However, he was paid only five dollars for the whole time and the food was very poor.

He tried for other jobs. "Let's see how well

you can write," said a shopkeeper one day when Davy asked him for work.

"I need a good boy, but he must know how to read and write," said a tavernkeeper.

Davy had to admit that he could do neither, and he had no time now to learn.

"I'll teach you a trade," offered a Mr. Griffith, "if you'll agree to work as an apprentice for me for four years. You'll live with me and when your time is up I'll pay you twenty-five dollars. What do you say?"

By this time Davy had learned the value of education and wished that he had gone to school. He decided the best thing to do was to learn a trade, so he agreed to Mr. Griffith's terms.

Davy tried hard, but he didn't like the work. He wanted to go back home to the wilderness, but he had become an apprentice and must do his best to learn the trade.

Luckily, Mr. Griffith was a good master. He

was kind to Davy and patient when he made mistakes, but he was not a good businessman. "I can't make money here," he said to Davy one day, about a year later. "I'm going back to Baltimore. You've been a good lad and I'll take you with me if you want to go."

"I don't have to go, sir?"

"No, I'll set you free from your apprenticeship. I have no money to pay you, though. I can't even pay the debts I owe."

Again Davy was on his own with no money. He was considered a good worker. Other men offered to take him as an apprentice, but Davy would not agree. He took whatever odd jobs he could find.

No matter how little money he made, he saved some. It took months to save enough to buy some decent clothes. Then he started home.

Davy was almost fifteen years old now. He had been away from home for nearly three years.

He had worked hard. Sometimes he had received good wages, sometimes no money at all. He had often been hungry. He had found some kindness, but he had also known loneliness and cruelty. He felt himself a man.

It was late fall when he reached Crockett's Tavern. Several people were waiting for the evening meal.

"Can I get supper and a bed for the night?" Davy asked his father in his man's voice.

"It will be fifty cents," Mr. Crockett answered. He hardly glanced at the newcomer.

Davy pulled out the coin and placed it on the table. He went over and sat on a bench along the wall, beside some others.

He sat there so quietly that men looked at him suspiciously. Frontier people were friendly. The stranger was supposed to be friendly, too.

Soon supper was announced. Davy went to the table with the others. Janie was sitting al-

most opposite him, but Davy didn't try to catch her attention.

"Bears are so fat this year, they roll like barrels," one man said.

"They sure do." Another laughed. "The only one I've seen all season knew he was too fat to run. He tucked his head in his paws, gave himself a push with a hind foot, and rolled downhill so fast my dogs couldn't get out of the way. He rolled right on top of old Rattler. Holdfast snapped all around him and couldn't find a corner to bite into. I got one shot, but the bullet couldn't pierce the fat. He went so fast I got dizzy, and old Music was baying in circles."

Davy spoke up, his eyes shining. "I aim to get a bear this year if I have to track him all the way to the end of time."

Janie looked at the strange boy closely, then jumped up and ran around the table.

"Davy!" she cried. "Ma, Davy's come home!"

172

Davy's First Bear

THE CROCKETTS were all delighted to see Davy again. His mother and sisters made a great fuss over him. They had been worried. They had heard no word of him since Bill had left him at Front Royal. Now Davy felt humble and ashamed to have caused his family so much anxiety while he was gone.

He thought a hundred whippings would have been easier to stand than the way he felt now. He wished he had gone to school. He still didn't know the first letter in the book.

Pa didn't mention the whipping Davy had so dreaded. His son was almost a man now.

"It's mighty late in the year to go bear hunting," Pa cautioned. "You had better wait until next fall."

"I'll go next year, too." Davy laughed.

"I've got a bee gum marked near the creek this side of Walton Ridge," said Wilson. "There are some big hollow sycamores up the hill. It's the right place for a bear to have a meal of honey and then crawl into his bed for the rest of the winter. Would you like to see what you could do there tomorrow, Davy?"

"I want to go, too," Joe said. He was a big boy, almost thirteen now. "I can shoot Sally Ann. I've kept her oiled and greased, haven't I, Pa?"

"Well," said Pa, "you can't shoot her as well as Davy could when he left home. But he couldn't have taken better care of her."

Davy eyed the dogs. "Where's Whirlwind? He saved me from a bear one time. I'll need him on the hunt."

174

"Whirlwind died of old age last winter, son. These young dogs haven't had much training. Maybe Zip Cochran will go along and take his Growler and Bearsnap."

Davy looked at the young dogs and then at his two brothers. "I reckon we can make out without Zip," he said.

The three boys with four dogs set out before daybreak the next morning. Wilson had Pa's rifle, Little Nancy. Davy carried Sally Ann. He noticed how carefully young Joe watched him. Davy remembered when Uncle Joe had let him carry a rifle. "I'll let Joe carry Sally Ann coming home," he thought. "And I'll give her to him when I'm through with her."

It was a noisy group. The dogs barked excitedly. Wilson blew on the cow horn he carried. Davy and Joe yelled. Before long the dogs raced ahead and the boys quieted down. Suddenly the dogs began to bay in the distance.

"Listen," said Wilson, "that's Soundwell. He's found the bear!" He sounded the horn again and the boys ran hurriedly toward the creek bottom.

There was the bear. He had been surprised as he climbed into the bee gum. Almost at the opening into the stored honey, he clung to the tree and glared at the noisy dogs.

Davy dropped to his knee and loaded quickly.

The bear climbed to a little limb to face the dogs and the boys. Davy circled to the right. There was no barrel rest. He must hold the long rifle at a high angle. Slowly he raised the rifle and sighted. With calm sureness he squeezed the trigger.

For a long moment after the crack of the rifle, the bear clung to the branch. Then he jumped or fell. The dogs leaped on him. His paws clawed wildly. One dog was badly raked. Then the bear lay still.

"You got him right through the heart like a streak of lightning!" Wilson shouted.

Davy patted his rifle. "Good old Sally Ann Thunder and Lightning," he said.

He handed the rifle to Joe and took out his hunting knife. Then he knelt and began to skin his first bear.

Remember the Alamo!

IN LATER years Davy was to kill many more bears in Tennessee. He became the state's best-known hunter, and many tales were told of his skill.

All his life Davy was a restless man. After he married, he moved again and again, taking his wife and children with him into the wilderness. From time to time travelers brought news about him back to his family at the tavern.

"Davy's shot all the bears in Lincoln County. He's moving again," one man reported once.

"Davy built a new cabin the other day," another said. "Did you hear about it?"

"Why did he move?" asked Mr. Crockett.

"Well, a hurricane blew his chimney over and the house burned down. Davy wanted to go hunting, so he had to built a new cabin in a hurry. He grabbed up his ax, ran a couple of miles to a chestnut grove and started cutting down trees. Every log he cut fell right in place on top of the one before to build the walls. The chips flew so high that they all landed in place for shingles on the roof as they came down. Then with his ax and his hunting knife Davy cut a door and two windows. It took him a little while to build the chimney, but he had a fire going and the latch-string out before supper."

Pa laughed. "Davy could do it if anybody could," he boasted.

Some time later another visitor brought news. "Davy has gone to fight the Indians with General Andrew Jackson," he said.

"I'm going too," announced Joe, the youngest Crockett boy.

When Joe came home he said, "Ma, everybody knows Davy. He always has a story to tell to make the men laugh. On scouting trips he hoots so much like an owl the Indians never guess there is a white man spying on them. And when he gives his turkey call the gobblers come from miles around."

Before long another traveler brought news to the Crocketts' tavern about Davy. "The men in the state militia elected him colonel," he said. "They voted for the man who could shoot straighter, and tell taller tales than anyone else."

Next someone brought news that Colonel Crockett had been elected a member of the state legislature.

"Why, he can't even read or write!" one old hunter said in surprise.

"Yes, he can," Wilson retorted. "When he came back from Virginia, Davy went to school four days a week and worked for the teacher the rest of the time to pay for his schooling. Davy's smart. He knows what he's doing."

Not long afterward a flood washed out Davy's new gristmill and powder mill and he lost everything he had. He decided to move to the Obion River, in western Tennessee.

"Why, that's earthquake country!" Mr. Crockett said when he heard the news.

"Davy says it's the richest land in Tennessee," replied the man who brought the news. "He says it has more bears than Daniel Boone ever saw."

The next thing the Crocketts heard was that Davy had been elected to Congress and was going to Washington.

"I bet he wears his coonskin cap and buckskins to call on the President," someone said.

All the old hunters in the inn laughed, but Mrs. Crockett said, "Davy knows when to wear hunting clothes and when to dress like city folks. Anyway, people will listen when he talks."

Altogether, Davy spent six years in Congress. When he was defeated in 1834, he became more restless than ever. Not even a good bear hunt interested him.

At that time everyone was talking about Texas. Texas was part of Mexico, but many people from the United States were moving there. Davy and some of his friends went to see this great new country to the southwest.

Davy liked Texas. He thought it would be good hunting and farming country. He liked the men who had moved there.

General Santa Anna, the president of Mexico, was worried because so many English-speaking people were moving to Texas. He made harsh laws to keep them out. When these did not succeed, he led his army against the Texans.

Everyone was excited. "The Mexicans don't want to live in Texas," frontiersmen said. "They just want to keep us out, but they can't do it.

182

We want to live here and we'll fight to stay, as free Americans."

General Sam Houston, a soldier who had fought under Jackson, was now living in Texas. He was told to organize an army to protect Texas from Santa Anna. He called for volunteers. He wanted to train a strong, well-equipped army.

Many of the frontiersmen had been Indian fighters. They wanted to fight the Mexican army in small groups, just as they had always fought the Indians.

"What are we waiting for?" they asked. "Let's go to meet the Mexicans. We can beat them any day."

"Where will they strike first?" Davy Crockett asked.

"San Antonio de Bexar," said one. "There's a fort there, with Colonel Bowie in command. The Mexicans will have to get past him before they can reach the rest of Texas."

"Let's go help him fight," Davy suggested to his friends from Tennessee.

All the men with Colonel Bowie were volunteers. Their fort was an old Spanish mission called the Alamo. Its walls had been strengthened and some cannon had been brought in.

Colonel Bowie was pleased to see the Tennessee men. "This is a key spot, but General Houston can't send us all the men we need," he said. "His army is still untrained, and he needs cannon and arms. He told me to retreat, because he thinks the Alamo cannot be defended. We think we can whip the Mexicans right here."

There were only one hundred and fifty men in Bowie's force, but each was an expert shot. "We can whip the whole Mexican army!" they cried. "Let them come. Victory or death!"

Then Bowie fell ill and young Colonel William Travis took his place. Travis called Davy in to talk with him.

"Colonel Crockett, you should have a command," he said.

"No, Colonel Travis, I was elected colonel, but that was just a compliment," Davy said. "When it comes to fighting I'm only a private. You can depend on Betsy and me to do a powerful lot of fighting, though." Betsy was the fine rifle friends had given Davy.

At last General Santa Anna with over a thousand soldiers reached the Alamo. He demanded immediate surrender and threatened death to every man who refused.

Colonel Travis answered his threat with a single cannon shot.

The Mexicans began to wheel their cannon into position before the Alamo.

Davy was standing at the parapet, watching. "That's a long rifle shot," he muttered. He raised Betsy to his shoulder and fired. A Mexican fell. A hunter handed Davy a loaded rifle. He fired again and another soldier fell. Once more Betsy was in his hands, reloaded. Shooting quickly, Davy dropped every Mexican gunner before any could reach shelter.

The Mexicans moved their cannon to more protected positions. They bombarded the Alamo for twenty-four hours. Travis sent a message to General Houston. None of his men had been killed and little damage had been done yet. He begged the General to send reinforcements.

"If none comes," he wrote, "it will be death or victory!"

Houston was still many miles away. He moved quickly, but he had little hope of reaching the Alamo in time.

Travis's men were hopeful. "We can hold out," they said, "and when our men get here——"

Scouts who had been sent for help came back, bringing thirty-two volunteers with them. They were the last who would come.

"It may be possible for men to slip out and make their way to safety," Travis said. He drew a line on the dirt floor. "All who will stay, step to this side."

"Be sure you're right and then go ahead," Davy Crockett thought. He was the first to step over the line.

Every man in the fort had known when he volunteered that it was a dangerous thing to do. Every man stayed.

For days the Mexicans were busy getting ready to attack. Santa Anna placed cannon to cover every angle of the fort. More and more Mexican troops arrived to help him.

There was little the frontiersmen could do. They kept an alert watch for Mexican scouts and spies, and picked them off one by one. They made every shot count. There was still no way to get more food or ammunition.

Ten days later Santa Anna was ready to at-

tack. Davy had been standing guard. Suddenly he shouted, "Here they come!"

The volunteers of the Alamo fought desperately for many hours. Every man had to fire and reload and fire again.

The gallant volunteers were completely outnumbered. The Mexican cannon knocked holes in the walls and Mexican soldiers swarmed through. Davy and a few others were driven back into the inner rooms of the Alamo. When their ammunition gave out, they used their guns as clubs.

Not a man surrendered. When the firing ceased only one person, a woman, was found alive in the Alamo. The Mexican general sent her back to General Houston.

"Tell Houston that everyone in Texas who refuses to submit to Mexico will be treated like the men in the Alamo," he said.

The woman told the story to General Houston,

who listened gravely. "Soon our army will be ready to fight," he said to the men around him. "When we meet Santa Anna, we sha'n't let him forget this. Remember the Alamo!"

General Houston was organizing his volunteer army and making his plans. Soon he would be ready to fight the Mexicans and win independence for Texas.

Around their campfires, his men told the story of the Alamo again and again. It always ended with the words, "Remember the Alamo!"

Some people could not believe that Davy Crockett had actually died.

"No Mexican bullet could kill him," they said. "He probably acted dead till the Mexicans were not looking. Then he whistled for Death Hug and left the Alamo."

"Who's Death Hug?" asked a stranger.

"He's the smartest bear in all creation."

"He's the bear Davy's little girl brought home

one time, and he just naturally took up with Davy," another man explained.

"Death Hug was smart. I heard they were out hunting one time and Davy ran out of bullets. A big party of Indians surprised them.

"Death Hug didn't need to be told what to do when Davy jumped on his back. He just clawed his way up the trunk of a big oak tree. He went so fast the Indians couldn't see where he was going. He scooted out on a limb and jumped like a squirrel to another big tree.

"Death Hug and Davy went away and left those Indians waiting with their guns all aimed to the top of the first oak tree."

"That reminds me of the time Davy was bear hunting in Arkansas," said another man. "He got word his oldest boy was sick. He wanted to get home in a hurry. So he whistled up a hurricane and grabbed hold of a streak of lightning. He greased it a little with some rattlesnake oil he had in his pocket. It let him down in his own backyard in nothing flat."

"All the animals knew Davy," said a tall hunter. "I'm from Tennessee, too, and I was there when he was elected to Congress. We had a big meeting and everybody voted. The people all cried, 'Crockett!' The little crickets chirped, *'Cr-k-tt-tt!'* The guinea fowls chattered *'Crk-kett—Cr-kt-kett!'* The bullfrogs came up from the creek to croak, *'Cro-o-cro-ock-ett.'* Even all the wild animals in the woods growled, *'Gro-gr-r-r-kett.'* "

"Do you suppose Colonel Crockett really could have escaped the Mexican army?" asked a serious young man.

The hunters all stared into the fire. They knew that Davy Crockett had not escaped the Mexican bullets. But they knew too that as long as men loved a tall tale, Davy would live in their stories.